B

Kelli studied Sam.

Nice suit. Made to measure, she was sure. Image was everything to corporate hotshots. Still, if she was objective, she had to admit the man was attractive, even more so when he smiled. His lips were drawn into a taut line now, which was a pity since he had such a nice mouth. It was a tad on the wide side, with a small scar just below the bottom lip that only added to his sensuality.

She coughed into her hand and glanced around the room. Where had such an improper thought come from? Samuel Maxwell was her boss. He was, now that she'd made the commitment to this game, her adversary. And if she were to win, which she certainly planned to do, she had to think of him as such. She could not afford to think of him as a man who had once caused her pulse to rev with a simple smile, no matter how sexy she found that little scar.

Jackie Braun began making up stories almost as soon as she learned how to write them down. She never wavered from her goal of becoming a professional writer, but a steady diet of macaroni and cheese during college convinced her of the need for a reliable income. She earned her bachelor's degree in journalism from Central Michigan University in 1987 and continues to work as an editorial writer for a daily newspaper. Fiction remains her first love. She lives with her husband and son in Michigan.

Working side by side, nine to five—and beyond....
No matter how hard these couples try to keep their relationships strictly professional, romance is definitely on the agenda!

Coming soon in the 9 to 5 miniseries:
Hired by Mr. Right
by Nicola Marsh
on sale February 2005, #3834, in Harlequin Romance®

Books by Jackie Braun

HARLEQUIN ROMANCE®
3804—HER STAND-IN GROOM

SILHOUETTE ROMANCE®
1479—ONE FIANCÉE TO GO, PLEASE
1599—TRUE LOVE, INC.

THE GAME SHOW BRIDE

Jackie Braun

TORONTO • NEW YORK • LONDON
AMSTERDAM • PARIS • SYDNEY • HAMBURG
STOCKHOLM • ATHENS • TOKYO • MILAN • MADRID
PRAGUE • WARSAW • BUDAPEST • AUCKLAND

For my "German girl," Linda Boeke,
exchange student extraordinaire.
I miss hearing you singing around the house.

ISBN 0-373-03825-9

THE GAME SHOW BRIDE

First North American Publication 2004.

Copyright © 2004 by Jackie Braun Fridline.

www.eHarlequin.com

Printed in U.S.A.

PROLOGUE

KELLI WALTERS was late for work again—half an hour late this time. She jiggled the fussy toddler on her hip as she slid her time card through the punch at Danbury Department Store's distribution center. To make matters worse, she was showing up for her shift with two kids in tow, one of whom was irritable and running a slight fever from teething.

"Remember, Katie, you need to keep Chloe with you in the break room," she reminded her seven-year-old. "You both need to stay out of sight until Mrs. Baker can pick you up."

That plan went up in smoke when Kelli turned the corner and ran straight into a man's broad chest. She stumbled back, an apologetic smile on her lips.

She didn't know the man by name, but she'd seen him the week before walking through the distribution center with one of the assistant managers. The instantaneous tug of attraction she'd felt then had caught her off guard. She'd chided herself for it, even as she'd returned the smile he'd sent her way.

And here he was again. Only this time he wasn't smiling.

"Sorry," she said.

He acknowledged her apology with a curt nod.

"What are those children doing back here?"

At the man's harsh tone, Katie slid behind her mother and Chloe sent up a wail of distress.

Kelli jiggled the baby and kissed her rosy, heated cheek. "It's okay, pumpkin. Don't cry." She transferred her gaze to the man. "Who exactly are you?"

"Sam Maxwell."

The name seemed familiar, although she couldn't quite place it.

"Ah, the new guy," she said at last, reasonably sure he was the distribution center's new manager, a position for which she had applied and never received even the courtesy of an interview.

Rumor had it that this guy was some shirttail relation to the personnel director, although Kelli didn't think he looked much like the short and bald Mr. Elliott. No, he was tall, at least six-two, with a full head of black hair and blue eyes that glared out from beneath a slash of dark brow.

He must be pretty full of himself, she decided, taking note of the nicely tailored suit he wore. Khaki pants and a button-down shirt would have been acceptable management attire in the warehouse. The suit was overkill and now it bore the unmistakable imprint of a child's runny nose just above the impeccably folded silk handkerchief that peeked from the breast pocket.

Serves him right, she thought none too charitably.

"New guy." He scowled. And then said dryly, "Yes, I guess I am the new guy."

Manager or no manager, handsome or not, he didn't need to upset her children.

"Well, Mr. Maxwell, did you really need to shout?" She tilted her head toward Chloe, who was still whimpering.

Dark eyebrows shot up over icy blue eyes. Clearly, he wasn't used to being reprimanded, especially from someone who obviously ranked low in the company's pecking order. Still, he lowered his voice when he said, "I asked a question. What are those children doing here?"

So, he was going to be one of *those* managers— the overbearing, inflexible kind who believed in following rules to the exclusion of all else. Employees weren't people with families and problems to this type of boss. No. They were automatons that needed to get the job done without asking questions or voicing complaints.

Unbidden and utterly inappropriate came the thought that it was a pity his good looks didn't extend to his personality. She brushed it aside, denying the attraction she had felt from that first glance across the room a week earlier. Her girls came first. They *always* came first.

"They're my kids. My sitter had a doctor's appointment this morning. She'll be here soon to pick them up."

"Soon? This is a business, not a day care."

She sighed in exasperation. As if that had escaped her notice. Kelli didn't know why she had expected him to understand or to care that even on good days being a single mother could be a trial. On days like this one, it was all she could do not to sit down and cry alongside her cranky toddler.

Chloe had kept her up most of the night. She was getting molars and wanted to ensure her misery had company. Of course, it hadn't helped that Chicago was in the grip of a major heat wave, making Kelli's fourth-floor apartment stiflingly hot. Two electric fans merely moved hot air around the small rooms, doing nothing to cool them. The coup de grâce had come that morning when the sitter had called. Kelli was ready to sell her soul for one hour of peaceful slumber in an air-conditioned room. Instead, she had eight hours of drudgery to look forward to and then an hour at home before heading to her night class. She'd be lucky to fall into bed before midnight and only then if she ignored the sink full of dirty dishes and mountain of laundry growing out of her closet.

"I'm aware that this isn't a day care," she replied, trying to keep her tone civil. "But I couldn't get anyone else. My backup sitter is out of town for a few days."

"Your personal problems are just that, personal. But they could become Danbury's problems if one of your children were to get hurt." He motioned with one hand toward the stacked pallets of inventory. "This is no place for children to be roaming around free."

"Roaming?" She sucked in a deep breath, swallowing an oath in the process. And to think she'd smiled at him on that first day. It only went to show how sorely lacking her judgment remained when it came to men.

Voice tight, she replied, "I promise to keep them on their leashes."

"And how can you do that and perform your job?" He didn't wait for her to reply. "You can't. Punch out and go home."

"Punch out and... Am I being fired?"

"No, but this will go in your personnel file. Now it's my turn to ask, who are you?"

So, the hotshot was determined to hone his reputation at her expense. Between gritted teeth she said, "Kelli Walters. That's Kelli with an *i*. Walters is the standard spelling. My middle initial is *A*."

"Well, Kelli Walters, you can consider this a warning. Bring your kids to work with you again and you will be punching out for good."

She was still gaping after him when someone said, "I see you made friends with Mr. Maxwell."

Kelli turned to find her co-worker, Arlene Hughes, standing behind her. Arlene was two decades older than Kelli's twenty-eight, with Lucille Ball red hair and the dramatically bowed lips to match. Despite the difference in their ages, the two women had been fast friends since Kelli hired in just after Chloe's birth.

"Mr. Understanding? Oh, yeah, he's going to be a load of fun to work for. He makes the last manager seem warm and fuzzy by comparison."

"He's not the new warehouse manager."

For the second time, Kelli found herself asking, "Who is he?"

"Samuel Maxwell. I believe there's a Third after his name. You know, the new vice president of Danbury Department Stores."

Kelli felt her mouth drop open, even as her eyes slid shut. Way to make friends and influence people. If she ever hoped to climb the corporate ladder at Danbury's once she earned her master's in business administration—assuming that happened at some point before she needed support hose and a walker—this was not the way to start out.

"Is he important, Mom?" Katie asked.

"Oh, yeah, Katie-did. He's really important."

"Well, I didn't like him," her daughter announced. "He yells. And he made Chloe cry."

"I think I might cry," Kelli mumbled.

She blew out a breath that caused her overly long bangs to stir. She needed a haircut and maybe some highlights to pep up the color of her mousy blond hair, but she had neither the time nor the money for such frivolous things. And that seemed to be the story of her life lately. No matter how hard she worked, she never seemed to get ahead. She felt like a hamster on a treadmill, only a hamster got to sleep all day. Kelli just had more running to do.

Anger and frustration bubbled to the surface. People like Samuel Maxwell *the Third*, who'd probably been born with a silver spoon in his mouth, would never understand what it was like to sacrifice and scrimp and do without and still wind up dodging creditors.

"I bet that man drinks bottled water, buys designer underwear and has his nails professionally buffed once a week. His kind wouldn't last an hour doing what we do day in and day out. He might get his hands dirty. Or his clothes."

She chuckled then, perversely pleased. "Oh my God! Just wait till he realizes he has baby snot on his pricey suit."

Arlene laughed, too, a great booming sound that had the Danbury's logo on her T-shirt bouncing on her impressive chest.

"He's awfully good-looking, though," the older woman mused. "Kinda reminds me of Pierce Brosnan with all that dark hair and those blue eyes. If I were ten years younger I wouldn't mind taking him for a tumble."

"If you were ten years younger and built like a *Playboy* centerfold he still wouldn't notice you. His kind dates humorless women named Muffy and Babs. He's too busy looking down his nose to really take notice of working stiffs like us. If I didn't need this job, I'd take him down a peg or two."

"Hey, you know what you should do?" Arlene didn't wait for her to reply. "You should go on that new reality show, *Swapping Places*."

Kelli rarely watched television. She simply didn't have time. "Never heard of it."

"It airs every Tuesday night. It's kind of *Survivor* meets *Big Brother* with a corporate twist."

"Sorry, I've never seen those shows, either."

Arlene shook her head in dismay.

"I know you take classes three nights a week, but what do you do for relaxation?"

"I sleep," Kelli said dryly.

"That's depressing, kiddo. You're young. You're in the prime of your life. You've got a nice shape, a pretty face. You should get out more. Date. Live it up a little."

"I have too many responsibilities to 'live it up.' As for dating, I'm not interested." She recalled the smile she'd sent Sam Maxwell the first time she'd seen him and her resolve hardened. "I don't need a man in my life."

Arlene sighed, knowing her protest was useless. This was an old argument. "Okay, at least hook up to cable or get an antenna so you can escape through television."

"I can't afford cable, and besides, the television works just fine with our old VCR. This way, the only things the girls can watch are the educational videos we check out at the library."

"If you go on *Swapping Places* you could win half a million bucks. That would buy a lot of educational videos."

"Yeah, well, I could win ten times more than that playing the lottery and the odds are probably better."

She shook her head. "No thanks. I'll make my money the old-fashioned way. I'll work hard and earn it."

"Oh, you'd earn it on *Swapping Places*," Arlene replied. "If Samuel Maxwell agreed to do the show, too, you'd be the vice president of Danbury Department Stores for an entire month."

Kelli stopped in her tracks. "Get out."

"I'm serious. Why do you think they call it *Swapping Places?*"

"And he'd be here in the distribution center, doing my job for the month?"

When Arlene nodded, Kelli snorted out a laugh. Glancing down at her callused hands, she said, "I'd almost pay to see that."

"More than just trading jobs, you'd trade lives. He'd be living in your apartment, taking night classes, making do on your budget."

"He'd be in my un-air-conditioned apartment, eating mac and cheese, dealing with backed-up sinks and leaky faucets while I'd go live in the lap of luxury for an entire month? Sounds like a dream."

Chloe began crying and the dream ended.

"So, what do you say? You want to do it?" Arlene asked.

"Oh, yeah. Sure," she replied with a roll of her eyes. "Sign me up."

Arlene cleared her throat. "I'm glad you feel that way, because I already did."

"You did what?!"

"I signed you up for *Swapping Places*," Arlene

replied as Kelli bounced Chloe on her hip. "I went on the show's Web site and typed in your name and information."

"When? Why?"

"A few weeks back. Right after you applied for the manager's job and didn't get asked for an interview."

"So, what, I'm supposed to go on national television and show Danbury's head honchos what I can do?"

"That was the general idea." Arlene shrugged. "But if you aren't interested, when the show's people call—*if* they call—you can simply say no."

"You'd better believe I'll tell them no."

CHAPTER ONE

Four weeks later

"Yes, I'll do it. I'll go on *Swapping Places*."

Kelli couldn't believe she'd said it, but she none-theless enjoyed the way her announcement caused Danbury's new vice president to blink in surprise. It didn't matter that at the moment the last thing she wanted to do was go on some reality television pro-gram. She'd think about that later and probably regret it. But right now she wanted to savor her victory, miniscule as it was.

She assured herself that her sudden willingness to participate in the show was only a matter of pride and had nothing at all to do with the fact that, arrogant and annoying as Sam Maxwell was, her pulse seemed to take off like a rocket whenever he glanced her way. Just nerves, she told herself.

And she *was* nervous.

They were seated in the company's conference room in the Danbury Building in downtown Chicago. Another time, Kelli might have enjoyed the swank surroundings and the killer view of Lake Michigan. But right now, she was still too tense. Her stomach had been knotted since receiving the call—summons really—from Samuel Maxwell the night before telling her to report to the main office the following morning. He hadn't given her a reason, but his tone had been no-nonsense to the point of sounding grave. She'd spent a nearly sleepless night worrying that she was about to be fired. She'd been late twice in the past week, after all. Now, she wasn't sure if being unemployed would have been so bad given what she had just agreed to do.

The legal counsel and assorted other representatives for *Swapping Places* sat on one side of the long conference table. Danbury's lawyers, Sam and his secretary sat at the other. One look at her frowning boss and Kelli had opted for the chair closest to the door when she arrived. For the past twenty minutes, the show's producer had done most of the talking and all of the pacing. Sylvia Haywood stood five-foot-three thanks to a pair of spike heels, but she stalked around the conference room with all the confidence and stature of a five-star general.

"You'll do it. Great!" She barely paused for a breath before she began ticking off the particulars of the show in a raspy voice that Kelli would bet was the result of smoking at least a couple packs of cigarettes a day. Then she paused and pinned Kelli with a flinty stare.

"You have kids, right?"

"Two girls."

"Hmm, that won't do."

Kelli gasped, startled by the woman's bluntness.

"Well, I'm not going to get rid of them just to do a television show."

"That's not what I meant." Sylvia paced again, running a hand through her spiky red hair. "You'd have to live in each other's homes, essentially take over all aspects of each other's lives. This works best with single people."

"I'm not married," Kelli said.

"Yes, but you have kids. How are you going to feel about leaving them in his care for a month?"

Kelli shook her head and without sparing a glance at her boss said, "Oh, no. Absolutely not. My kids come with me."

"That pretty much blows the whole point of the show. He needs to step into your shoes. You're a single parent. That has to cause a lot of stress and create a lot of challenges for you, especially since you work full time and take night classes."

"You have no idea," Kelli muttered.

"No, Ms. Walters, *he* has no idea." Sylvia pointed at Sam.

"Well, I'm not leaving my kids in a stranger's care."

"Ms. Walters, a camera crew would be there most of the time," Sylvia said. "And, if it would make you feel more comfortable, you could get your sitter to move in for the duration as long as she stayed in the background and didn't perform any actual child-care duties. Your girls would be safe and well cared for."

"No. My daughters are my responsibility."

Sylvia sighed. "Could they go stay with their father for a month?"

It embarrassed Kelli to admit, "I don't know where he is."

"You don't know where he is? What about child support?" Sam asked.

They were the first words he'd spoken since she'd walked into the room. His tone wasn't critical. In fact, his expression seemed to be one of concern. Still, Kelli bristled. It reminded her just a little too much of how disposable she and the girls had been to her ex-husband.

Kyle had left without a backward glance while she was still pregnant. He'd never even seen Chloe. The last time Kelli had come face-to-face with him was in a courtroom when they had divvied up their limited assets and dissolved their marriage. He hadn't sought joint custody or even visitation. He'd simply said goodbye.

"I heard that he moved out of state not long after Chloe was born." She didn't add that he'd done so with the college-age girlfriend for whom he'd tossed aside nine years of marriage.

For the millionth time, Kelli told herself it was Kyle's loss. She didn't need him. The girls didn't need him.

"You should have someone track him down," Sam persisted. "I can put you in touch with a good attorney."

Pride had her lifting her chin. "I'm perfectly capable of providing for my children, thank you very much."

"I wasn't implying that you weren't. But as their father, he has a responsibility to—"

"Responsibility?" Kelli issued a humorless laugh. "Believe me, that's not a word in Kyle's vocabulary."

"I've got it! I know how we can make this show work," Sylvia interrupted. And Kelli found herself thankful for the woman's one-track mind. "We'll have to bend the rules a bit, but I think it would add an interesting twist that our viewers will enjoy."

"Bend the rules how exactly?" Kelli asked.

"You could spend the weekends with your kids, unless there's a work function that requires your attention. We probably won't use much of the tape from then anyway, but Mr. Maxwell would have to be included. And he'd have to handle household tasks as well as any crises that came up. As for during the week, you could slip back into the apartment around midnight, as long as you're gone by eight the next morning."

Sam straightened in his seat. "Um, and where will I be?"

"I'm assuming she has a couch," Sylvia replied, one eyebrow arched. "You'll have to stay."

Kelli swallowed hard, but at least had the satisfaction of seeing Sam do the same.

"He c-can't stay in my apartment," she stammered. "What would my girls think?"

"She's right. It wouldn't look...appropriate."

"That part wouldn't be broadcast to America," Sylvia said. She laid her palms flat on the table and split an exasperated gaze between the pair of them. "Look, we're all adults here, so this shouldn't be a problem. You're not lovers, for crying out loud, and this show is not *Temptation Island*. So, take it or leave it. This is the last concession I'm willing to make."

Of course they weren't lovers. They hardly even knew one another and what Kelli did know about Samuel Maxwell the Third, she didn't like. Still, a man in her apartment overnight?

"I don't know," she said.

"The payout is half a million dollars, Ms. Walters. You need to look at the big picture here."

Kelli glanced at Sam. Sylvia had already explained that if he won, the television show would make a sizable donation to the charity of Danbury's choosing. But he didn't really have anything to lose. Either way, Danbury's would still receive all that wonderful free publicity. What would she get if she lost? Sylvia seemed to read her mind.

"You're taking night classes, right?"

"That's right. I'm working toward my master's degree in business."

"This could be the best chance you'll ever get to prove your potential in management. Consider it an internship. Better yet, consider it a way to broadcast your résumé to every company coast-to-coast. You could wind up a very hot property afterward, Ms. Walters. The last winner was interviewed on *Good Morning, America* and the *Today* show, not to mention making the cover of *Time*. Even the loser wound up doing *Oprah*."

Kelli had to admit, her career path at Danbury's was not looking particularly promising, and not just because the personnel director was hiring family and ignoring her applications. She glanced over at her glowering boss and took a deep breath.

"Okay."

Sylvia nodded briskly. "We'll assign a camera crew to each of you for the duration. You'll have some privacy—bathroom, some financial stuff, it's all spelled out in the folder I've provided—but everything else will be on the record. Not all of what we tape will air. It will be edited down to the salient points. You'll have to sign a legal waiver, of course.

"You may ask each other for help or advice, but points will be deducted." She glanced between them. "And not that this should be a problem, but too much cooperation and you will both be disqualified."

As she went on, Kelli studied Sam. Nice suit. Custom-made, she was sure. A fit that perfect didn't come off the rack. And those broad shoulders were probably the work of a clever tailor rather than a gym membership. Image was everything to corporate hotshots. Still, if she was objective, she had to admit, the man was attractive, even more so when he smiled.

His lips were drawn into a taut line now, which was a pity since he had such a nice mouth. It was a tad on the wide side with a small scar just below the bottom lip.

I wonder how he got that?

Contact sports? A barroom brawl? Neither seemed likely. Whatever the cause, the scar only added to the sensuality of his mouth.

She coughed into her hand and glanced around the room. Where had such an improper thought come from? Samuel Maxwell was her boss. He was, now that she'd made the commitment, her adversary. And if she was to win, which she certainly planned to do, she had to think of him as such. She could not afford to think of him as a man who had once caused her pulse to rev with a simple smile, no matter how sexy she found that little scar.

She coughed again.

Was the woman coming down with a cold? Sam wondered. That could work to his advantage. He was beginning to think he'd need all the advantage he could get. He sat across from Kelli, lounging in his chair and hoping he looked bored and unconcerned, but he was starting to wonder what he had gotten himself into. Swapping places hadn't seemed like such a big deal when they had actually been, well, swapping places. But now they would be sleeping under the same roof. Separate beds or not, he didn't like it. He liked his space and his privacy. Yes, that was why the arrangement had him so unnerved.

But as he clicked the pen he held in his hand, and studied Kelli Walters, a question nagged him. What was it about her that intrigued him so much? She was attractive, but with her unstyled hair and serviceable fashion choices, she certainly wasn't as polished or poised as the women who usually drew his attention.

He inventoried her features—stubborn chin, high cheekbones, slightly upturned nose, and chocolate-colored eyes. Maybe it was those eyes that pulled at him. They held a hint of vulnerability, but Sam knew firsthand she was no pushover. She didn't back down. She held her ground even when she had plenty to lose. Grudgingly, he admitted he admired that.

He recalled their first meeting, which really couldn't even be called a meeting. Sam had seen her as he'd toured the warehouse with a group of managers. She'd been checking in inventory with her back to him, slender legs and slim hips neatly packaged in denim. Forget the fact that he was Danbury's vice president and acting CEO, only a blind man would have failed to appreciate the view, and his eyesight was twenty-twenty. Then she had straightened and stretched with catlike grace, tilting her head side to side as if to work out some kinks. When she'd turned and caught him looking at her, he couldn't help but smile. And she'd smiled back—seeming shy, interested and slightly irritated all at the same time.

Even if the company had not had a no-fraternization policy, their second meeting would have snuffed out any possible flirtation. The distribution center already had failed one Occupational Safety and Health Administration inspection. The inspectors were due back the day Sam had run—literally—into Kelli and her kids. Maybe he could have gone a little easier on her. He'd certainly ruffled her feathers, which he supposed was for the best. Again, his mind returned to the disturbing thought that he would be sleeping on her couch for a month.

Click-click-click! Her boss held the pen like a dagger, his thumb depressing the top at regular intervals. Was he nervous or just irritated?

Ultimately, Kelli decided, it didn't matter. The show of emotion told her he was human. It told her that he could be riled and shook up by life's curve balls. Well, he'd be thrown plenty of them once he stepped into her shoes. When her gaze traveled from the pen to his face, she discovered he was watching her.

He merely raised one dark brow, but she felt her face heat to be caught staring. At least that's why she told herself she blushed. Surely it had nothing to do with the fact that he really did resemble the debonair actor Pierce Brosnan. Throw in an accent and he'd be a dead ringer. Throw in the accent, she mused, and she and half the females in Chicago would be a puddle of mush at his feet. Thank God he sounded like the East Coaster he was.

Eye contact seemed to stretch interminably. Sylvia Haywood's gravelly voice thankfully broke the spell.

"What do you say, Mr. Maxwell? Do you think

you can handle Ms. Walters's life for an entire month?''

His gaze cut to Kelli again, this time far more arrogant than considering.

"Her life for one month?" He shook his head as if insulted. "When I win, make the check out to the American Cancer Society."

Kelli was halfway to the elevator when she heard Sam call her name. She was tempted to pretend she didn't and just keep walking. *When I win,* indeed. The man was insufferable. But she stopped and turned, crossing her arms over her chest as she waited for him to reach her.

"Is there something you wanted to say to me?"

"Oh, plenty."

"I see. Well, can it wait till I punch back in? I think I'd prefer to listen to you when I'm getting paid for the privilege."

He scowled. "My office is this way."

He walked away without another word, obviously expecting her to follow, which she did reluctantly, mumbling oaths under her breath as she went.

His office was just as she would have imagined it to be: large, with imposing cherry furnishings and cold leather upholstery on the high-backed chair that was his highness's throne. There were few personal touches—no photographs of loved ones, plants, plaques or little gadgets with which one could waste time when bored or perplexed. The room revealed little of Samuel Maxwell's personal nature, which could mean he was an intensely private man. Or perhaps it revealed that he didn't have much personality once one got beyond his uncompromising countenance and sexy mouth.

"Nice office," she said with a smirk, telling herself it was the latter.

He glanced around. "It serves its purpose."

"Ah, the no-nonsense type."

"You'll find, Ms. Walters, that there's not a lot of time for nonsense when you're running a business."

He sat on his throne and she wanted to crown him.

"You'll find, Mr. Maxwell, that when you're raising children, you have to make time for nonsense."

"We'll see about that."

"Yes, we will." She sat on one of the chairs in front of his desk. "So, what did you want to talk to me about?"

"I want to assure you that your employment will not be in jeopardy regardless of the outcome of the show, nor will this affect any opportunities you might have for advancement within Danbury's."

"Now, that's a relief."

"Is there a reason for your sarcasm?"

"No, sir. I'm sure any future promotions for which I apply will be given the same consideration as the last one."

He frowned at her. "The last one?"

"I have to get back to the distribution center.

We're a little short-handed today,'' she said as she got to her feet.

"They'll survive a little longer without you." He motioned for her to sit back down. "I just want to make sure you know that even though you'll be in way over your head, the rest of the management team will be here to hold your hand."

He sounded sincere, which only made his words all that more patronizing.

"So, I'll be in way over my head, hmm?"

"A few business classes, even at the post-graduate level, don't prepare one for running a national chain of department stores."

"You've been studying my personnel file."

"That is my prerogative as your employer. But no, I haven't been studying it. I merely glanced at it when I added the warning about bringing your children to work."

"So much for family-friendly workplaces," she muttered.

"OSHA wouldn't agree with your definition of family friendly, Ms. Walters. In fact, its inspectors were on the way to the distribution center the last time you decided to get creative with your day-care accommodations."

The explanation of his surly behavior that day did little to alleviate her irritation. "Haven't you ever had a bad day?"

"Our days are ultimately what we make of them— good, bad or otherwise. Organization is the key."

She folded her arms across her chest and leaned back in the chair. "So, now I'm disorganized?"

"I'm merely pointing out that you obviously have some flaws in your system if one or two little glitches can throw your life into chaos."

"Life, Mr. Maxwell, is not a system, and children are not a glitch." When he opened his mouth to speak, she held up a hand to silence him and had the pleasure of watching one of his dark eyebrows rise in pique. "Nonetheless, I'll be curious to see how you manage when you experience a few 'glitches.'"

Oh, his day was coming, all right.

"Are you assuming that every day is a holiday when you're in management?"

"Not at all. But all the well-thought-out systems and procedures and policies in the world won't work on a teething toddler who won't sleep or a seven-year-old who's convinced there are monsters under her bed."

"Are you trying to make me nervous?" He looked amused by the prospect.

"Of course not. I'm trying to make you aware that being a parent, single or otherwise, is full of challenges. There are no instruction books, no one-size-fits-all solutions, no management teams to consult. Half the time, you've got to think on your feet, even when you'd rather be soaking them in hot water because you've been standing on them for the past twelve hours."

"So, being a parent is all drudgery."

She couldn't help but smile, thinking about the big messy kiss Chloe had given her that morning and the crayon-drawn invitation Katie had presented her for tea later that evening.

"I suppose I made it seem like that, but not at all. Parenthood has unimaginable rewards. Even on those bad days, I wouldn't trade my kids for anything. They're…they're…" She groped for the right words, but none seemed adequate. So, she settled on, "They're what make it all worthwhile."

When he said nothing, just continued to regard her with an expression she couldn't quite read, she stood.

"Now, I really do have to get back to work. Some of us get paid by the hour."

Sam dismissed her with a nod, but long after Kelli Walters left his office, he sat in his chair, thinking about what she had said.

Thinking and remembering.

The old hurt bubbled to the surface, and he let it come until it spilled over him as destructive and relentless as molten lava. He knew better than most that life was not a system. It was unpredictable, messy. Well-laid plans and, with them, futures could be shattered in the time it took to say goodbye.

From his wallet he pulled out the photograph his mother had included in her last letter. She wrote to Sam at least once a month. He never wrote back, although he did call on occasion. None of this, after all, had been her fault. He stared at the photo as he had a dozen times since receiving it a week earlier.

Two adorable boys dressed in their Sunday best smiled back at him. Their dark hair was neatly combed, but mischief sparkled in their blue eyes. Maxwell eyes.

They were five and three now and the delight of their doting grandparents, but Sam had never met them. They were his brother's sons, but they should have been his—just as Donovan's wife should have been Sam's.

CHAPTER TWO

"WHY are we cleaning the house on a Thursday? Saturday is cleaning day," Katie complained as she dusted the coffee table.

"I told you, Mr. Maxwell will be here in an hour, along with the television people. I'm not going to have them thinking we live like slobs."

The meeting would include the show's host, a slick-talking former MTV veejay named Ryan O'Riley, and the camera crew that would follow Sam. On Saturday, Kelli would meet her camera crew at Sam's house. She could only imagine the kind of luxury the vice president of Danbury Department Stores lived in.

Kelli glanced around her apartment, trying to see it from a stranger's point of view, trying, she admitted, to see it from her wealthy boss's point of view. The blue sofa with contrasting pillows and the overstuffed floral chair were too big for this miniscule living room. Of course, they'd looked charming in the cozy house she'd shared with Kyle. Kelli hadn't been able to afford the mortgage after he'd left. In fact, as it turned out, they hadn't been able to afford the house together. Her ex-husband had been paying the bills using credit cards. So, she'd sold the house, and a good deal of its furnishings.

But the apartment didn't look bad. She'd always had a knack for decorating—large spaces or small. She'd hung white linen panels that she'd made herself at the double window. They helped to conceal a rather uninspired view of the fire escape. At an art fair the previous summer, she'd splurged on a pair of dreamy watercolor seascapes. On the opposite wall, she'd hung a set of white box-shaped shelves she'd found at a rummage sale. She hadn't had to make them look distressed. They already were. Pictures of her girls, framed in simple blue or white wood, graced one shelf. Three of her favorite teacups from her collection stood on the other. The total effect was a bit French country, a bit flea market.

Her one extravagance, if it could be called that, was the red rose she placed in a small bud vase in the middle of the coffee table. At the first sign of wilting, she bought a new one from the flower shop two blocks from the apartment. She'd started buying the roses right after Kyle left. They represented hope. And they reminded Kelli to take time not just to smell a bloom's sweet scent, but to appreciate the beauty that could be found in unexpected places—like a perfect flower in a stuffy, small apartment or the gurgling laughter of a sticky-faced toddler.

With fifteen minutes left before her company was to arrive, Kelli was coaxing Chloe to eat the remainder of her macaroni and cheese. If she got lucky, a

Sesame Street video might keep Chloe occupied for most of the meeting. Katie could be counted on to entertain herself as well as see to any of her little sister's immediate needs. It bothered Kelli sometimes that Katie had so much responsibility heaped on her small shoulders. Cleaning house and tending to a toddler shouldn't have been regular chores for a seven-year-old. But Katie rarely whined about it. Like her mother, it appeared she had already learned the futility of complaining.

The doorbell rang just as Chloe decided to dump her plate of gooey pasta over the side of the high chair.

"All done!" she announced proudly as the food hit the floor Kelli had just scrubbed.

"Chloe Elizabeth! We don't throw our food."

The toddler only grinned. "No, no, no," she said as she shook one chubby finger.

"Mom, someone's here," Katie called from the doorway.

Nerves fluttered in her stomach.

"It's probably Mr. Maxwell or the people from the show. Can you let them in, please? I need to clean up in here and then I'll be right there."

Sam hadn't expected a child to open the door. The young girl he'd seen that day at the warehouse stared up at him. She was a miniature version of her mother, with the same chocolate eyes, same upturned nose and same stubborn chin lifted in defiance. Yes, it was going to be a very long month.

"Hello. I'm Mr. Maxwell. I believe your mother is expecting me."

"I know. I'm Katie. Mom said to let you in. I'm supposed to be nice to you, even though she thinks you're a jerk." Her eyes grew wide and he waited for her apology, but she said, "Don't tell her I said that, okay. I'm not allowed to say jerk."

Sam coughed. The girl was indeed her mother's daughter.

"We'll keep it between the two of us then."

Katie motioned for him to come inside. The apartment was small, but tidy, and just this side of blast-furnace hot. He'd hoped, prayed actually, that the ride up in the elevator had been an aberration. But the fact became plain. The building did not have air-conditioning, and neither did this small apartment. It was mid-August, which meant it could be a good month before the weather turned cool.

Then Kelli Walters walked into the room, and he would have sworn the already ungodly temperature inside the apartment notched up another dozen degrees. Sam had been sure this bizarre and unsuitable attraction had run its course, but clearly it hadn't.

What was it about her?

Her hair was pulled back in a simple and youthful ponytail; her skin was dewy with moisture. She wore a yellow tank top and tan cotton skirt that stopped a good three inches above her knees. There was nothing overtly sexy about the casual outfit and he supposed it made sense given the heat, but Sam wished she'd worn slacks. The woman had some nice legs—as slender as a model's and yet as toned as an athlete's. He tugged at his tie and unbuttoned his collar.

"You might want to slip off your jacket before you pass out," she said wryly. "It's a bit warm in here."

He dragged his gaze away from her legs. "Warm? Oh, no. Hot. Extremely hot."

Awareness seemed to hum between them for a moment before she said, "No air-conditioning, sorry."

She pushed a stray lock of hair off her damp forehead, looking not the least bit apologetic. "Can I get you something to drink? I've got iced tea."

"Anything cold would be fine."

As Sam said it, he felt a tug on his pant leg. He looked down into the messy, orange face of a grinning toddler.

"I remember you," Sam murmured, thinking about his last run-in with the baby. He'd had to send his jacket out for spot removal. If her hands were as messy as her face, it looked like he could count on another dry-cleaning bill.

Kelli glanced down as well and then gasped. "Chloe!"

She transferred her sheepish gaze to Sam. "I'm sorry, Mr. Maxwell. I was so busy wiping up the mess she made on the floor I never got around to her hands and face. She's become a regular Houdini lately. Even when I buckle her into the high chair, she can manage to slip out."

"I'll keep that in mind."

He took his handkerchief from his pocket and wiped at the streaks around his right knee, succeeding only in making a larger smear.

Kelli had just managed to clean up the toddler when the doorbell rang again. She ushered all of her guests into the cramped living room and, after ensuring that the girls were settled in their bedroom with a video, she returned with a tray of glasses and a pitcher of iced tea.

The only available seat was on the couch next to Sam. Their knees bumped as she settled onto the half of a cushion that remained.

"Excuse me," they both said at the same time.

Kelli crossed her legs in the hope of making herself somehow smaller, but she only succeeded in making her skirt smaller. The hem hiked up to the middle of her thighs. As she tried to discreetly tug it back down, Sam reached for his iced tea, nearly draining the glass before putting it back on the tray she'd set on the coffee table.

"Can I get you something else?"

He responded with a curiously tight, "No."

For the next half hour, Joe Whaley, the main cameraman who would be assigned to Sam, explained what he would and would not film. After a quick tour of the apartment and a brief introduction to Kelli's girls, he decided where remote cameras would be positioned.

He was a big burly man, with shaggy dark eyebrows and a tattoo of a dragon on one bicep. Yet, he'd gotten down on one knee to shake hands with Katie and had even managed to delight a laugh out of Chloe with his impression of Donald Duck.

After he stood, he asked his young assistant, "What do you think, Nic? How many remotes do you figure this job will take?"

"Four? No, five, Dad."

He gave her ponytail an affectionate yank and winked at Kelli and Sam.

"She's a chip off the old block," he said with obvious pride.

Any concerns Kelli had about leaving her kids with Sam while under this man's watchful eye evaporated. Joe was a father, and her gut instinct told Kelli that tattoos or not, he was a good one.

Back in the living room, Joe explained to Sam, "While at work and outside the apartment, one or two cameramen will follow you, but I'll be your main man."

"Looking forward to it," Sam grumbled.

Ryan piped up then. "Sylvia asked Ms. Walters to write out a schedule of sorts for you. Of course, you don't need to follow it to the letter. One of the points of the show is to improve on the other's routine. That can mean using time or money better than the other person."

"Efficiency is one of my specialties." Sam sent Kelli a superior look that set her teeth on edge.

She enjoyed watching his smug smile falter a bit when she handed him a dozen single-spaced, typed pages of instructions, most of them having to do exclusively with her children.

"Pages one through three deal with the basics, like dinner menus, bed and bath times, what books we've been reading before going to bed. Sitter information. That kind of thing."

Just for good measure she asked, "You know how to change a diaper, right?"

"I think I can figure it out."

"I go grocery shopping on Monday evenings after class because the lines are shorter and Mr. Kennedy, he's the butcher, gives me a good deal on the meat that's getting near its sell-by date."

When he raised an eyebrow, she reminded him, "My bank account is a lot more limited than yours and that's what you'll be living on for the next month."

"Fine. So you shop on Mondays when the meat is cheap and near spoiling."

Pride had her lifting her chin. "That's right. I also try to cook for the week that night after coming home from class. You can get two meals, sometimes three, from a whole chicken if you do it right. Of course, you're a bigger eater than any of us. There might not be much meat left for your soup."

"It comes in a can, you know."

"I like it homemade. Besides, this is cheaper and more nutritious. A sliced up stalk of celery, diced carrots and onion, and you've got a meal at half the cost. I add dried basil to the broth for extra flavor."

"Anything else, Emeril?" he asked snidely.

"Katie's allergic to peanuts. It's a serious allergy, so you have to read all food packaging carefully. Sometimes different batches of the same product can be cooked in peanut oil. If you eat out, not that I expect you will be doing much of that on my budget, stress to the waitress the importance of nothing with peanuts or peanut oil coming into contact with her food."

"What will happen if it does? Hives?"

"She could die, Mr. Maxwell," Kelli said bluntly, and watched his expression turn sober. It was just the reaction she was hoping for. He needed to be well aware of the seriousness of this matter.

"Her throat will swell, constricting her air passage. I keep an emergency hypodermic of medicine in the apartment as well as one in my purse. You probably should carry one as well."

He straightened in his seat. "I'd have to give her a shot?"

Kelli nodded. "And quickly. You can't just call 911 and hope paramedics make it here in time to perform an emergency tracheotomy. I'll show you how to give it. You can practice on an orange if you'd like." She paused, her tone deadly serious when she asked, "Can you handle this?"

The enormity of what she was asking him to do struck Sam with the charged force of a lightning bolt. Kelli quite literally was entrusting him with her children's lives.

Trading places had seemed relatively uncomplicated until this point, even with the two of them sleeping under one roof. Making meals, reading bedtime stories, he wasn't looking forward to spending time with children, but one didn't need a PhD to handle that. Deadly allergic reactions, however, were a whole other matter.

For the past six years, Sam had studiously avoided thinking about what kind of father he would make— would have made had things turned out differently. His own father had been firm and somewhat distant, paying the bills and offering his approval on rare occasions. Sam's mother, a nanny and the teachers at his boarding school had seen to the details.

But when he stepped into Kelli Walters's single-parent shoes, there would be no one else to whom he could relegate those details. It would all come down to him for an entire month.

"Yes or no?" she asked.

She was sitting next to him on the couch, her gaze unwavering. He didn't realize he'd reached for her hand until he felt her fingers grip his.

"Yes." He squeezed hers in return as he added the phrase he had not uttered to a woman in more than six years. "I promise you."

With some regret, Kelli left her girls with the sitter Saturday morning and hustled not to be late for her hair and makeover appointment. If nothing else, she mused, she would get a much-needed haircut and highlights out of this experience. Not to mention some great clothes.

The show had tried to talk her into going to a chic salon and some of the designer shops on Chicago's famed Michigan Avenue. But Kelli had held firm in her conviction that as the acting vice president of Danbury's Department Stores, she would use the people, the products and the clothing available there.

It was her first decision as acting vice president and CEO, and she believed it set the tone for her brief tenure. She wanted to ensure that consumers who normally did not shop at Danbury's would give the store a second glance after watching the show.

A camera crew filmed her transformation from the first snip of hair and stroke of mascara to the point when, sleekly coifed, she stepped into a pair of stylish leather heels that cost nearly as much as two weeks' worth of groceries.

She barely recognized the image that stared back at her from the dressing room's large tri-fold mirror. Her hair had been highlighted and cut even with her chin, managing to look professional despite the sassy little flip it did at its ends.

Her makeup was slightly more dramatic than if she had applied it herself, but the effect brought out her high cheekbones and gave her eyes an almost exotic quality.

And her clothes…

She smiled and did a little turn to admire them from all angles. She'd opted for something a little trendier than classic. The short peach skirt with its flirty, ruffled hem wasn't exactly her style, but she liked the tank-style tangerine sweater that had been paired with it, as well as its matching cardigan. She decided if she went too conservative, she might give younger viewers the impression that Danbury's was still their grandparents' department store, not the place they could go for fun outfits and accessories.

A consultant from the television show helped Kelli pick out a couple dozen different outfits for work and day wear as well as three evening gowns and a couple of cocktail dresses. She'd balked at first. Did she really need so much? But after some persuading and with someone else picking up the tab, she finally got into playing Cinderella.

An hour after the last of her purchases had been boxed up for delivery, she found herself—in a limo no less—being whisked to Sam's home in a gated community in the suburbs of Chicago that boasted its own exclusive golf course.

The house was as big as she had imagined it would be and looked recently built, judging from the size of the shrubs and staked trees that dotted the landscape. The house was what was called a story-and-a-half, with a tall, pitched roof and lots of big fancy windows that screamed high energy bills. She'd bet her paycheck it was at least 4,500 square feet of living space.

Sam answered the door himself and Kelli had the satisfaction of watching his mouth drop open when he saw her new look.

"Something the matter?" she asked, unable to keep her smug smile in check.

"I haven't decided."

"Indecisive? You? Hmm. I thought you had everything figured out."

She was flirting with him and they both knew it, but she couldn't seem to help herself. It had been a long time—a very long time—since she'd felt young and attractive.

She thought she heard him murmur, "So did I."

"Are you going to let me in or do I have to stand out here in the heat?"

"You come in and it won't be much cooler in the house," he replied. Still, he stepped aside to allow her to enter.

He was flirting with her as well, she realized.

He didn't look much like a powerful executive today. In place of a tailored suit, he wore a pair of faded jeans and a short-sleeved polo shirt. His feet were bare. And while he was no bodybuilder, his arms were far more muscular than she would have guessed and the broad shoulders were definitely authentic. Urbane, physically fit and mentally agile. Arlene had pegged him right: Sam Maxwell was Pierce Brosnan as James Bond.

"You clean up amazingly well," he said.

They stood in the foyer, a step too close together, and yet Kelli didn't back away. She should have put an end to this inappropriate byplay, but like a moth drawn to the danger of a flame, she couldn't quite bring herself to do so. If it was part of his strategy to win, she wanted him to know that two could play his game.

Surely that was the only reason she let her gaze flick down to his bare feet and back up before replying, "And you dress down well. I wouldn't have guessed you owned jeans."

"We're even then. I wouldn't have guessed you owned high heels."

"Oh, I'm full of surprises," she said.

"I'm beginning to think so."

He reached out, and for a moment she thought he might stroke her cheek, but he drew a ribbon of her hair between his index and middle fingers instead, following its length to the freshly snipped ends.

"You cut your hair."

The breath seemed to back up in her lungs and it took an effort to squeeze out the words, "Yes, among other things. What do you think of my makeover?"

"I'm not sure I can think."

If this was mere flirting, it had taken on a dangerous edge. And still, Kelli did not back away. In fact, she moved forward ever so slightly, testing this new power she seemed to have. Testing herself.

"Come now, a man of your immense control and mental fortitude? I find that hard to believe." She allowed a smile to slowly lift the corners of her mouth.

"Are you sure you want to know what I really think?" The space between them grew perilously meager as he stepped forward, all but pinning her between his body and the equally unyielding wall.

"Yes."

The breathy whisper seemed to come from a stranger. Kelli wasn't sure she knew herself anymore. She certainly could no longer fathom her motives for baiting such a powerful and not always pleasant man.

But she watched his mouth, that sexy, tempting mouth, as he replied, "Then, I'll show you."

With his hands flat against the wall on either side of her head, he leaned in. Nothing but their lips touched, but that was more than enough. The kiss was as ruthless as she knew he could be, and yet it made her heart race even as her mind became sluggish and muddled, unable to process anything but taste and texture and undeniable pleasure.

The doorbell rang, but he lingered over her mouth for a moment longer before stepping back. He trailed a finger down her cheek before lifting her chin.

"Rule number one in business, Ms. Walters, never let down your guard. It gives the competition too much of an edge."

So, it had all been a game. Kelli didn't know whether to be relieved, disappointed or angry. As she watched him open the door for the camera crew, his expression steeped in satisfaction, she found that she was all three.

CHAPTER THREE

THE KISS had been a bad idea.

And even so, Sam found he wanted to do it again. Thank God for the doorbell or who knows how far out of hand things between the two of them might have gotten. He wasn't a man ruled by passion, and yet he'd barely managed a coherent thought when he'd opened the door a few minutes earlier to see Kelli standing there, looking pretty and fresh and, yes, sexy.

This time, to his relief, the people who stood on his doorstep merely looked miserably hot and impatient. He ushered them inside and led everyone to what the real estate lady had told him was the hearth room when she'd sold him the home.

House, he corrected himself. There was nothing homey about the huge rooms, most of which were still empty. Much of the furnishings from his place back in Connecticut just had not seemed right for this one. So, he had employed an interior designer to fill up the rooms with furniture, wall hangings and shelves dotted with the kind of useless bric-a-brac and whatnots that made a house looked lived in. The hearth room, off the kitchen, was the only room that had that quality.

"Can I get anyone anything? I have iced tea, soda,

spring water,'' he said as the camera crew and Ryan settled onto the two supple leather couches that faced one another in front of the fireplace.

Kelli, he noticed, had stopped to look at the artwork that hung on one wall. Or maybe she was just trying to keep as much distance as possible between the two of them. That theory went up in smoke a moment later when she followed him into the kitchen with an offer to help him with the beverages.

"Let's get one thing straight, Mr. Maxwell,'' she hissed once they were out of view and earshot.

"I think you should call me Sam, under the circumstances,'' he interrupted.

"Sam,'' she gritted out between clenched teeth, "I don't know what you were trying to pull back there, but this is business. If I were a man, you wouldn't have kissed me.''

"No,'' he agreed. And then couldn't resist baiting her some more. "Of course, a man wouldn't look like you do wearing a skirt and heels.''

She closed her eyes, and he got the feeling she was counting to ten.

"Look, ultimately this may be a game, but I'm taking it very seriously. I have two kids to support. I need the money if, *when* I win. So, there are some rules.'' She held up a single slim finger. "Rule number one. Keep your hands off me.''

"Technically, I think it was our lips that touched. In fact, I think my hands stayed on the wall the entire time.''

"Are you being purposely obtuse or are you really this slow? If so, I shouldn't have a problem winning. In any case, keep your lips to yourself as well. I shouldn't have to spell this out for someone working at the executive level in corporate America today."

The subtle reminder that he was treading on dangerous legal ground snapped him out of his strange mood. She was right, of course, and showing a lot more sense than he was at the moment.

He cleared his throat. "I'm sorry. I've acted inappropriately and it won't happen again."

She gave a jerky nod to accept his apology, obviously deciding he was sincere. And because he was also a gentleman, Sam opted not to mention that her response to his kiss had been anything but cool and professional.

The tour of Sam's house took more than two hours as the camera crew debated the best places to put the remotes. Sam had explained that he was still in the process of furnishing the house with the help of a professional, but Kelli itched to offer suggestions anyway. The high ceilings, the arched windows, the lovely woodwork—there was so much to work with here.

Even so, it surprised her when he said, "The interior designer will be here again Wednesday evening. She's bringing some wall hangings for the great room and some fabric samples for the furniture and window treatments. Since you'll be here, I'll leave that to you."

"You trust me to decorate your house?"

"Why not?"

"I'm practically a stranger."

He shrugged. "So is the interior designer."

When she continued to stare at him, he said, "Look, it's my fourth house in six years. I've hired out the decorating in all of them with pleasing results. Besides, with my work schedule, I'm rarely here to do more than sleep anyway."

"Why did you buy a house this large if you obviously don't need the space? They make one-bedroom apartments, you know."

"It's a good investment," he replied. "A good tax shelter."

They seemed sad reasons to buy a big house. And so even though it was absolutely none of her business, she heard herself ask, "What about family? Don't you plan to have kids someday? You've got four bedrooms, not including the master suite. Plenty of room for them to—what was the word you used?—ah, yes, *roam* free."

His expression clouded and he said tersely, "I don't plan to have a family."

"I'm sorry."

She wasn't apologizing for bringing up such a personal subject, but rather for his decision to never become a father. And the look he sent Kelli told her that they both knew it.

* * *

Late that afternoon, once he was alone, Sam picked up the telephone. A moment later, Stephen Danbury, president and heir to the department store chain that bore his family's name, came on the line.

"Keeping things running smoothly, I presume."

"Smooth is a relative term in business," Sam replied wryly. "We're issuing a product recall on a toy sold exclusively through our stores, and OSHA's fining us for a violation the inspectors found during their last visit to the warehouse."

"Ah, things are about the same, I see."

He chuckled softly. "Yeah." And because it seemed the polite thing to do, he asked, "How's the family?"

There was a smile in Stephen's voice when he replied, "Good, very good. Galena gained another pound."

Stephen and his wife Catherine had welcomed their daughter a couple of months ago. Sam had known Stephen for a few years, although not well before coming to Chicago to take the position that Stephen's cousin had previously held. Still, it seemed hard to reconcile this doting dad with the stoic CEO he remembered. Envy was a rare emotion for Sam, but he recognized it as what he felt. He could have been this happy, this content, if things had worked out differently.

Kelli's question came back to him. *Don't you plan to have kids someday?*

Once upon a time he had looked forward to fatherhood. He'd looked forward to growing old with Leigh, his high school sweetheart. They had dated throughout college, even though they had attended different universities. They'd talked about a future together long before he'd made their plans official with an engagement ring. And then it was over. His bride had walked down the aisle of the church that June, but the groom had been Sam's brother.

Annoyed with himself for wallowing in such unpleasant memories, he got down to business.

"Everything is all set for Monday. I'm still not sure this is a good idea, but I do plan to win."

"That's good to know, but the company comes out ahead either way."

A baby gurgled in the background and Sam would have sworn he heard the once no-nonsense Stephen Danbury blowing soft raspberries. Another time, it might have made him smile. But he found himself irritated.

"Well, anything for the company."

"You're okay with this, right?" Stephen asked. "When we spoke about it earlier, you seemed convinced the benefits for the company would be worth the huge personal imposition this will mean."

Imposition was too sanitary a word. His involvement in the show promised to be a down and dirty competition, and Sam had no one to blame but himself. An entire month of nights in Kelli Walters's stifling little apartment wouldn't have been such a big deal if she weren't also in close proximity. Now, he would know she was there, mere feet from where he slept, wearing heaven only knew what to bed. What had he been thinking, kissing her that way today?

"Your silence is making me nervous," Stephen said with a laugh.

"I'm fine with this, really. I'll just be glad when it's over."

"I've told you already how much I appreciate the sacrifice, but it bears repeating. *Swapping Places* could very well prove to be a gold mine of free advertising for Danbury's. Our marketing department just doesn't have the resources right now to generate this kind of coast-to-coast publicity without seriously harming other parts of the operation. You know as well as I do that Danbury's continues to teeter on the edge financially."

"Well, this should ensure we resonate not just with the older consumers who have been our bread and butter, but the younger ones with all of their disposable income."

"I owe you for this," Stephen said, his tone serious.

Sam shifted in his seat, uncomfortably aware that the company's best interests and bottom line had not been the only things on his mind when he'd committed to do the show. And they certainly had been nowhere on his personal radar screen when he'd kissed Kelli that afternoon.

First rule of business: never let down your guard. Well, he'd busted it handily all by himself.

Monday morning came before Kelli was quite ready for it. She showered and then changed clothes three times before settling on a beige linen suit and a pair of open-toed shoes whose heels were an inch higher than she felt were sensible. But they looked great with the outfit and kept it from being overly conservative.

The sitter knocked on the door as she was applying lipstick—a color called cinnamon apple that the sales woman had assured Kelli went perfectly with her warm skin tone.

Before leaving, she stood in the doorway to the girls' bedroom as she always did. This time, though, she hesitated longer than usual. Chloe was on her back in the crib, her little bow mouth slightly parted and a halo of damp ringlets around her chubby face. She wore a diaper and nothing more because of the heat, and Kelli couldn't help but think she looked like a cherub. Lord knew, when she was awake, that wasn't always the case.

Katie slept on her belly, half of her face obscured by the pillow, blond hair fanning out behind her. The ends needed a trim and Kelli wondered if Sam was any good with a pair of scissors. She'd leave him a note.

"I love you girls," she whispered.

The overwhelming sense of it no longer surprised her, but it still did cause her eyes to mist. Her girls were two bits of perfection that had come out of utter failure, which was why Kelli would never regret her marriage to Kyle.

She wouldn't see the girls today. Not until after midnight when they were once again sleeping in their beds. It wouldn't be the first time that had happened, of course. But that didn't make it any easier. Once she finished night school and if she were to win this contest and if she could land a good-paying position...

"Things will be different soon," she quietly promised them.

"You'd better get going, Kelli," Mrs. Murphy called softly from behind her. "It's quarter to seven."

Outside, a soft, misty rain fell, all but evaporating before it hit the hot pavement. Kelli opened her umbrella and stepped out of the doorway of her building, intending to walk the five blocks to the El stop. She noticed the camera crew first, and then she saw the sleek black limo.

"Good morning, Ms. Walters." A man in a black cap hopped out from the front seat. She recognized him from the previous Saturday. He'd been the one to chauffeur Kelli to her appointments and Sam Maxwell's house.

"Good morning, Milo."

He jogged around the front of the car to open her door, smiling as he came. The camera crew followed. She glanced at them, resisting the urge to fiddle with her hair. Then, acting as if it were every day that she rode to work in a limo, she climbed into the back and settled onto the supple leather seat. She might have relaxed then, but Vern, her main cameraman, waited inside, sitting just opposite her.

"Just act natural now. Pretend I'm not here."

"Um, sure."

The window that divided the inside of the car slid open.

"There's coffee in the carafe to your right, Ms. Walters. Mr. Maxwell takes his black, so I just left it plain. But once I know your preferences, I'll be sure to have it made right. Sugar, creamer and cups are in that little compartment," he added, pointing.

By the time they'd pulled away from the curb, Kelli had a cup of coffee in one hand and a copy of *Business Week* in the other, and she was doing her best to act natural despite the fact that a camera lens followed her every sip and page turn.

For the first time in years, Sam overslept. He'd hit the off button instead of snooze on his alarm clock and by the time he awoke, he had just fifteen minutes in which to shower, shave and dress. Hair still damp, he jogged down the stairs wearing jeans and the short-sleeved shirt with the Danbury logo that all distribution center employees were required to wear.

Joe and his daughter were waiting by the door for him.

"Running a little late, huh?" Joe grinned and didn't wait for a response. "Tomorrow, of course, you'll be able to sleep in a little since you'll be at Ms. Walters's apartment in the city.''

"No need to remind me," Sam muttered. He glanced at the equipment, then at Joe and Nic. "Hate to tell you this, but Kelli has the limo and my car is a two-seater."

"It doesn't matter. You don't get to use it for the next month."

"How am I supposed to get to work?"

"Today, I'll drive you in. Tomorrow you'll be leaving from Kelli's house, so it's the El for you, pal."

"Public transportation?"

Joe just grinned.

At the warehouse, Sam punched in with just seconds to spare, and then only because Joe had denied his request to stop for coffee.

"I'm Arlene," a plump middle-aged woman said, her red lips bowing into a smile as she divided a glance between him and the camera crew. "I get to show you the ropes."

Sam hadn't had his first cup of coffee yet and was dying for some caffeine, but when he mentioned this fact to Arlene, she shook her head.

"Sorry, hon. First break isn't till ten o'clock and no food or beverages are allowed out of the break room. Company policy."

"Of course."

He'd have to talk to Stephen about having that changed, he thought grimly.

* * *

Kelli took a moment to enjoy the sensational view of Lake Michigan from Sam's office window as she sipped her coffee, her third cup of the morning. The secretary, Lottie Branch, had brought it to her when she'd inquired about where she could get a cup. This was better than the thick brew the machine in the warehouse's break room managed.

"You have a marketing meeting in five minutes," Lottie reminded her and then paused to glance at the cameraman that Kelli had almost managed to forget was there. Clearing her throat, Lottie added, "I've typed up some notes that hopefully will bring you up to speed."

Lottie was no-nonsense and obviously efficient, even if she wasn't a particularly warm woman. Indeed, she had yet to crack a smile. Kelli had no idea what she thought about this bizarre situation. The woman could clean up in a poker game with that stoic expression. But something told Kelli that Lottie's loyalty to the company would be to her benefit.

"Thank you."

The morning did not go well. Sam didn't like to admit it, but Kelli's job was not only physically demanding but challenging in other ways as well. Some tasks were tedious and repetitive. Others, time-consuming. All of them seemed thankless despite their obvious value to the overall operation. And since he knew what Kelli was paid, he had to wonder what made it all worthwhile. Of course, he knew that her income was just as good here as it would have been as manager of some retail store. And, of course, the hours were better. Still, she was bright, obviously motivated. This job seemed a little too much like settling. And he said as much to Arlene.

"She's not settling. She's determined to make a name for herself in business. But her kids come first. This job might be a no-brainer, but she gets to pull a straight day shift Monday through Friday. That means she gets the weekends with her kids and can go to night class."

Sam knew it was none of his business, but he found himself asking, "What about her ex-husband?"

"I didn't know him." Arlene shrugged. "But he had to have been a jerk. He left Kelli before Chloe was born. He's never even seen that little angel."

Sam didn't want to feel sorry for Kelli, and he certainly didn't want to admire her. But he did. She was a survivor, a fighter. Those weren't traits he often associated with women. Or at least with the kind of women he was attracted to. Since his breakup with Leigh, Sam had preferred females who were a little...helpless. Women like his current girlfriend, Celine Matherly.

They'd begun dating shortly after he arrived in Chicago, but Sam wouldn't have termed their relationship serious. And if they were still dating a year from now, he wouldn't consider it serious even then.

Still, he enjoyed Celine's company, and she wasn't without her charms. She looked phenomenal in an evening gown—and even better out of one. She was the kind of woman who accepted his long hours without complaint and when she attended a business function as his escort, he never had to worry about her saying something foolish or controversial. She had the art of small talk down to a science, and if the conversation wasn't particularly stimulating, well, other aspects of their relationship certainly were.

She wasn't particularly pleased that he was doing the show, especially once she found out he would be playing house with another woman. But he'd managed to make her forget about the arrangement the last time they were together.

He glanced at his watch. Time for lunch. Given the sort of the day he'd had, he needed the distraction a beautiful woman could provide. For some reason, the image of Kelli Walters interrupted his thoughts.

He pushed her from his mind as he dialed Celine's number from the phone in the break room.

"What are you wearing?" he asked when she came on the line.

"Hello, Sam." Her voice was a sexy purr, nothing at all like Kelli's even tone. "Did you wake me up just to find out my clothing choice?"

"Wake you up?" He consulted his watch. "It's lunchtime for us working stiffs."

"Yes, well, some of us like to lounge in bed."

"Is that an offer?"

"It could be."

"You never did tell me what you're wearing."

She issued a throaty chuckle intended to tease his libido.

"Why don't you come over and find out for yourself? I'll treat you to…a late lunch."

"That's the best offer I've had today. But we'll have to make it another time. I'm punching the clock, remember?"

"How can I forget?" He knew she was pouting. "I hardly saw you before. Now, I'll be lucky to see you at all for an entire month."

It didn't seem like such a hardship to Sam, but he wisely kept that observation to himself.

"We'll spend a night on the town when this is over," he promised. "Dinner, the theater, the works."

"I'll look forward to it," she replied.

"Me, too."

The response was expected and appropriate. He'd said similar things to a dozen different women over the past six years. But for some reason this time it bothered Sam that he didn't mean it.

Kelli had three meetings and two conference calls before lunch, which made her suspect Sam had packed his Monday morning schedule on purpose. But, she'd handled them reasonably well, or at least she thought so. What counted, of course, was what the show's judges thought.

She called home twice to check on the girls, something she did even in her job at the warehouse. Mrs.

Murphy assured her they were fine, but then Katie got on the phone.

"When are you coming home, Mom?"

"You know the answer to that one already, Katie-did. I'll be home at midnight, long after you're in bed."

"And *he'll* be here."

"Yes, *Sam* will be there to make dinner. And I want you to behave for him."

"But I don't like him. Do you like him, Mom?"

Of course she didn't like Sam Maxwell. So, she had responded to his kiss. It meant nothing. It was on the tip of her tongue to agree with her daughter, but then what kind of an example would she be setting as a parent?

"Be good for him, Katie. And help with Chloe, please. He doesn't know a lot about babies."

"Just come home now. Me and Chloe will be good."

"Chloe and I." She mumbled the correction automatically, even as her heart twisted. "And I know you will be good. This isn't punishment. Be my big girl, please."

"But a month is so long," Katie whined.

To a child an hour could be a long time, but in this case, Kelli had to agree with her. "I know, sweetie. But it will be worth it. I promise."

CHAPTER FOUR

SAM wanted nothing more than to twist the top off a cold beer and tune in to the Cubs game when he got home. Instead, when he walked inside the stiflingly hot apartment, he had to make dinner. And he had to do it on camera, as if he were filming a segment for *The Frugal Gourmet*.

He opted for something simple that wouldn't hike the temperature in the apartment any higher than the ungodly inferno that it already was. Peanut butter and jelly, he decided, before remembering Katie's peanut allergy. He eyed the stove. Grilled cheese. He was capable of making grilled cheese. Katie, of course, critiqued his every move.

"Mom cuts off the crust. We don't like crust," she informed him with a roll of her eyes.

He complied with her wishes.

"When it's on the plate, she doesn't cut it in half. She cuts it into four little triangles."

He'd already cut one in half. "This one will be mine," he said before gritting his teeth and doing as she instructed.

But if he'd thought Katie was going to be the hard one to please, Chloe appeared determined to outdo her older sister. She fussed throughout dinner, chanting, "I want my mommy," half a dozen times before finally throwing most of her mangled sandwich onto the floor.

Afterward, Sam had barely enough time to clean up her mess before the sitter arrived and he was heading out the door for his first night of class at Northwestern University.

Kelli would be taking this semester off. She'd balked a little. Still, he thought she must have been a bit relieved with the reprieve. And, after just one day in her shoes, he couldn't blame her. He wouldn't admit it to anyone, of course, but her schedule was challenging.

Sam wouldn't be earning credit for the graduate level course, but he was expected to pay attention, scribble down notes and take any quizzes or exams the professor administered that first month. He figured it would be a piece of cake. He was the vice president and acting CEO of a major department store chain, for pity's sake. He knew how to run a business. He didn't bother to pull out a pen or paper during the hour-long lecture, and he had a tough time keeping his mind from wandering and his eyes open. Joe, who sat next to him yawning as he held the camera, was of no help at all.

It was during the ride home on the El that he realized he'd forgotten to do the grocery shopping. Well, it would have to wait until the next day.

* * *

Kelli had plenty to keep her busy, but she watched the clock, wishing away the minutes until she could return to her small apartment and her sleeping children. She'd resisted the urge to call again. Katie's words still haunted her.

I don't want to be a big girl.

And Kelli couldn't blame her. Katie was seven. She shouldn't have to act like an adult, but too often that's what was expected of her. A tear slipped down Kelli's cheek. She brushed it away, hoping the ever-vigilant camera had not caught her show of weakness.

Picking up her pen, she returned to the stack of paperwork on the desk before her.

At the stroke of midnight, Kelli was sliding the key into the lock, eager to see her children and hoping to tiptoe past Sam without disturbing him.

What did he sleep in?

The thought had her pausing before turning the key. She hoped he slept in more than the Jockey shorts her ex-husband had preferred. Her traitorous mind took an inappropriate turn and conjured up a vivid picture of a nearly naked man glistening with perspiration, sprawled on the couch of her sweltering apartment.

Swallowing hard, she pushed open the door. I'm not going to look, she told herself, even as her gaze veered to the right.

There was indeed a man on her couch and he was probably sweating profusely given the fact that he wore a pair of conservative long-sleeved striped pajamas. He was on his back, one hand flung over his head, feet dangling over the far end of the couch. God, he looked incredible. *Uncomfortable,* she corrected herself. He looked incredibly uncomfortable.

She closed the door, flipping the dead bolt, depressing the lock on the knob and finally sliding the security chain into place. When she turned, he was sitting up on the couch.

"Sorry, I didn't mean to wake you," she said.

He ran a hand through his hair, leaving it mussed, and somehow making the scene seem more intimate.

"I wasn't sleeping."

"Oh." She hesitated awkwardly just inside the doorway as the silence stretched. "How was your day?"

"Fine. Yours?"

"The same. The girls give you any problem?"

"None. Meetings go okay?"

"Fine."

They eyed one another like a pair of boxers in the ring.

"Well, it's late. Good night."

"Good night."

Sam watched as she walked down the hallway. A few minutes later, he listened as the water ran in the bathroom. First the sink and then the shower. A few minutes later, he heard her bedroom door click shut and his imagination took off, pulling his libido along with it.

Sam shrugged out of the pajama shirt he'd put on for her benefit, but he kept on the pants.

As he laid back atop the sheet on the sofa, it was his turn to wonder what Kelli wore to bed.

He learned the answer to that a few hours later when Chloe sent up a wail of distress. To Sam, the high-pitched screech sounded like a siren. He bolted off the couch, disoriented until he remembered where he was and why he was there. He stumbled toward the back bedroom at the same time Kelli emerged from her bedroom.

She stood in the hallway wearing a pair of gray cotton jogging shorts and a skimpy pink tank top. She might as well have been wearing the latest creation from Victoria's Secret with the way his body responded. Her hair was tousled, her face scrubbed clean of makeup and the brief excuse for sleepwear was wrinkled, but she looked as sexy as a lingerie model. Only the remote camera mounted on the hallway wall kept his mouth from dropping open.

"Baby's crying," he mumbled, but neither of them moved. Her gaze, he noted, had dropped to his bare chest. "Uh, it's pretty hot in here. I took off my shirt. Do you mind?"

She didn't speak, merely shook her head. Chloe wailed again.

"I'll get her," Sam said. "Technically, it's my job. Remember, you're not supposed to be here."

She nodded before returning to her room.

Sam lifted the squalling toddler out of her crib. Katie, he noticed, was sound asleep, not disturbed in the least by her sister's banshee cry, which told him that this was probably a frequent occurrence. And he still had the better part of the month to go. He sighed.

In the dim light of the hallway, Chloe blinked up at him, and then shrieked even louder. Uh-oh, Sam thought, this might be a very long night.

"Hey, it's not as bad as all that," he whispered, giving her back an awkward pat. He'd never comforted a crying child before.

"I usually rock her for a few minutes until she settles down."

He turned to find Kelli standing in her doorway.

"Mama," Chloe sobbed, holding out her chubby arms.

"I can rock her," she offered, taking the baby.

Sam stood there, feeling a little helpless as he watched Chloe stop crying the instant she was lifted into her mother's arms.

But he was a man of principle. He wanted to win, he *would* win, and he would do so fair and square.

"No. I'll rock her. Where's the chair?"

Kelli tilted her head toward the open doorway. "It's in my bedroom."

"Oh."

He followed her into the small room. It smelled like Kelli: the scent feminine and floral. Her perfume, he assumed. He hadn't been inside this room yet. He considered a woman's boudoir off limits, unless he was invited inside. He reminded himself this invitation was hardly the sort to raise one's ardor, especially since they were chaperoned by a sniffling, wide-eyed toddler. Even so, he swallowed hard when Kelli sat on the edge of her rumpled bed.

The room was sparsely furnished, which was good since it was so small. The double bed was pushed against the far wall, a dresser with the usual female gadgets and whatnots on top occupied a good portion of the rest of the room. The mirror that hung on the wall behind it had a few pictures tucked into the frame—Chloe, Katie and an older couple Sam assumed were Kelli's parents. The rocker was next to the bed, separated only by a small table. The lamp on top of it was switched on low, creating a disturbing sort of intimacy.

Time to get down to business. He held out his arms for Chloe.

"Come here, kiddo, we're going to rock," he said briskly.

Kelli chuckled as the baby burrowed closer to her chest.

"She's a toddler, Sam, not some errant employee. You haven't been around children much, have you?"

The image of two blue-eyed boys came to mind, followed swiftly by guilt. But he had nothing to feel guilty for, he reminded himself. *Nothing*.

His tone was brusque when he replied, "Not much, no."

"Well, they respond best to gentle tones." She arched her eyebrows meaningfully. "That's especially the case at this age and younger. Do you know any songs?"

Sam scratched his chin. He was a U2 fan, and he liked Matchbox Twenty, Hootie and the Blowfish, and the ageless sound of the Beatles and Simon and Garfunkel. But he didn't think that was what she had in mind. "As in lullabies?"

She nodded.

"Not really."

"I guess it doesn't matter what you sing, as long as it's got a slow tempo."

She stood and motioned for him to sit in the rocker. When he was seated, she settled Chloe onto his lap. The little girl's face scrunched up and Sam braced for another ear-splitting wail, but Kelli forestalled it with a pacifier she pulled from the small drawer in the top of the bedside table.

"You might have told me about that a little earlier," Sam said dryly.

"I'm trying to break her of it, but desperate times…" She smiled wearily, motioning toward the alarm clock. It was nearly four in the morning.

"No need for both of us to be up. Why don't you go sleep on the couch for what's left of the night?" Sam said. "I think I can take it from here now that the secret weapon is in use."

Kelli hesitated, and he wondered if she would object. She seemed to have such a hard time delegating duties, especially when it came to her kids. Finally, she stood, apparently having decided to take him up on the offer, but by then Chloe had other ideas.

She began whimpering again and tried to scoot off Sam's lap.

"It's okay, sweetie. Mommy's not going anywhere." She sent Sam a resigned smile and sat back on the bed.

"Might as well make yourself comfortable," he said when she made no move to lie down.

It seemed surreal that he was in a woman's bedroom, coaxing her to go to sleep rather than trying to coax her out of her clothes. Of course, this *was* Kelli Walters. He wasn't here to seduce, but to win. She stretched out on the mattress and then rolled to her side. Long, sleek legs bent at the knees, and she tucked her hands beneath the pillow. For just a moment, he questioned his priorities.

Both females eyed him expectantly. And though Sam was rusty, he started to hum the Beatles' "Yesterday."

One corner of Kelli's mouth lifted in what he decided was appreciation, if not for his musical talent, then at least for his sense of irony. So, he began to sing about a time when trouble was far away, humming the phrases he couldn't quite remember. He rocked slowly in the chair, its gentle creak and the sounds of traffic outside the open window the only accompaniment as he patted Chloe's back in tempo to the song.

Kelli had thought Sam attractive before, whether wearing a suit or a pair of old jeans. But the sight of him bare-chested, holding Chloe, rocking and singing softly had something shifting inside her, mellowing, melting. He's playing to win, she reminded herself, recalling the kiss that had made her weak, that had made her want things she hadn't wanted in so long. It was all about strategy. And yet she wondered, could he be that cold, that calculating? Could he hold a sleepy toddler who gazed up at him with such trust, such innocence, and not feel the need to nurture and protect?

She closed her eyes and called herself a fool. Hadn't Kyle already answered that question for her? Hadn't he taught her that some people could walk away from love and from the people that love had helped create? And still it niggled at her as sleep beckoned. Kyle had never held Katie the way Sam was holding Chloe just now. He'd never sung either of his daughters to sleep.

Kelli awoke just before her alarm sounded. She rolled to her side and glanced at the clock, and then noticed Sam, who was still sitting in the rocker holding Chloe. Both of them were asleep, and judging from the angle of Sam's neck, he was going to be stiff. A smile tugged at her lips. She'd fallen asleep in that chair often enough to know exactly how he would feel when he finally woke up.

As if he sensed she was there watching him, his eyelids flickered open. Even in the room's dim light his gaze was potent when it locked with hers.

"Good morning," she whispered. Then she sat up. Something seemed far too intimate about wishing him a good morning while her head was still on the pillow.

"You can put her back in her crib now," Kelli said, nodding toward Chloe. "She'll probably sleep for another couple of hours. If you get really lucky, she won't wake up before the sitter gets here."

She frowned.

"What?"

"Of course, then you won't get to see her until tonight."

"It bothers you, doesn't it? Not getting to spend a lot of time with your kids."

"I think it bothers most working mothers. My schedule is so crazy right now, and of course the show has made it even worse since I'm not allowed to come back to the apartment until midnight. But I keep telling myself it will be worth it. I'm doing it for them. Someday, things will be different." She flashed a rueful smile. "I just hope that happens before they graduate high school."

The alarm sounded then and she quickly hit the off button.

"And the rat race begins again," he teased, wondering at the ease with which they regarded one another this morning. He should have felt awkward, waking in her bedroom, holding her baby in his arms.

Instead something about the scene felt oddly right.

"So it does. Of course, I do get to sleep in the limo on the way back to your house. And, being an executive and all, I don't have to start work until an hour after you do."

"Go ahead, rub it in," he grumbled.

She took him at his word. "Did I mention the coffee that Lottie makes? And the croissants and fresh melon she'll have waiting for me at the office?"

Kelli stood and watched his gaze travel the length of her legs. There was no mistaking the interest she saw there.

"You're just cruel," he whispered, and she got the distinct impression he was talking about more than her mention of croissants and cantaloupe.

She sauntered toward him, her gaze never wavering even though her heart pounded in anticipation. She couldn't believe what she was about to do.

"Do you think I'm cruel, Sam?"

She leaned over the rocker, bracing her hands on the armrests. Her face was mere inches from his, and she was fully aware that the pose afforded him a rather liberal view of her cleavage. She had the satisfaction of watching him swallow hard.

He didn't say anything, just watched her with those impossibly blue eyes.

"I'm not cruel, but I am smart."

She leaned forward, nearly touching his lips before changing direction and dropping a light kiss on Chloe's forehead.

He expelled a ragged breath as she straightened.

"First rule of business, Sam. Remember? Never let down your guard."

She sent him a wink over her shoulder as she walked to the bathroom. And because she couldn't help herself, she started to hum "Yesterday."

CHAPTER FIVE

THAT almost kiss haunted Sam for the better part of the morning, so much so that Arlene finally had to tap him on the shoulder to gain his attention and tell him it was time for a break. He needed something stronger than the black, bitter coffee the break room's machine dispensed to clear his head. But he tossed it back anyway, grateful for the caffeine.

"So, how is single parenthood?" Arlene asked. She sat across the small, scarred table from him, her ruby lips spread into a knowing grin.

Sam couldn't help but like the woman. She didn't tiptoe around him or treat him like displaced royalty. So many of Kelli's other co-workers did. Still, if she thought he was going to admit he faced a tough adversary as Joe sat nearby with a camera, she was mistaken.

He shrugged. "Her life's not easy, but then neither is mine."

To himself, of course, he was willing to concede that Kelli's life was far more hectic and demanding than he had imagined.

As a salve to his ego, he rationalized that he'd been dropped into her circumstances cold. Big changes like this took some getting used to—for all parties concerned. The kids didn't know him or trust him—they didn't necessarily even like him. Chloe eyed him stoically, her unblinking gaze unnerving. And Katie, as independent and headstrong as her mother, wasn't willing to give him the benefit of the doubt on anything. Her subtle and not-so-subtle criticisms over everything from the way he'd made grilled cheese sandwiches to the way he'd scrubbed the frying pan afterward had him second-guessing himself. Sam would have never dreamed that a seven-year-old could so successfully nick his self-confidence.

He was the acting head of one of the country's oldest department store chains. He had a law degree, a business degree, and he'd graduated in the top ten percent of his class from Harvard. He'd always assumed he was reasonably good with people, able to make friends and win over adversaries without too much effort. But it seemed he'd met his match with Kelli and her girls, which made him determined to try that much harder. It was the challenge that tugged at him. Certainly, it wasn't the prickly woman or her precocious progeny.

Still, in the wee hours of the morning, when he'd rocked with Chloe and felt her finally lay her trusting head upon his shoulder, Sam had felt something he'd never felt before. He thought about the picture of two smiling boys that he carried in his wallet. Perhaps he would have experienced it if Leigh and Donovan hadn't betrayed him.

He blamed the bitter taste in his mouth on the coffee.

"Time to get back to work," he said, standing abruptly.

Arlene eyed him in bafflement. "Hold your horses, pal. We still have another nine minutes of break time. Believe me, you don't want to rush these things."

He tossed the paper coffee cup into the garbage can. "See you back on the floor."

At noon, Kelli and Sam met with Ryan in Danbury's conference room where a light lunch had been set up. The day before, since it had been the first day of the switch, they had individually filmed sound bites that would be shown on the premiere episode of *Swapping Places*. Today, they would officially begin their daily meetings with the show's host to discuss their strategies and discover who was faring the best according to an unseen panel of judges watching the video.

They eyed one another stoically, the morning's events sizzling between them.

Kelli licked her lips in nervous anticipation, her competitive spirit kicking in. The contest had just begun, but she wanted to start out ahead and stay there. A come-from-behind finish might have more drama and flair, but she wanted the edge of confidence that went with front-runner status.

"It's early yet, but so far both of you have managed quite well in each other's lives. The stakes are high, of course, half a million dollars is on the line."

The handsome host turned to Kelli. "Not a bad pay-out for a month's work, huh?"

When she only smiled, he motioned for the camera to cut off.

Ryan was Kelli's age, but he seemed so much younger to her in his hip clothes and pricey sneakers. A little silver hoop dangled from one ear and his smile was boyishly charming, but he took his position as show host seriously.

"Come on, now. Both of you are sitting there like statues. This is television, not radio. We need to see some facial expressions. We need to see some animation. Talk a little trash. You know, get on one another's nerves."

"That's easy enough," Sam muttered.

"That's it, that's it." Ryan grinned. "Remember, this is a competition, not a tea party. You're playing to win, not to tie. You know, take no prisoners, go for the jugular."

He made it sound like a blood sport. Nonetheless, Kelli tried to do as instructed and found it easier than she thought once Sam began to offer his bland commentary on her life.

They bickered back and forth for the better part of the hour. When the meeting ended, they were glowering at one another and Ryan looked smug and satisfied.

Kelli let herself in to Sam's house. Vern had packed up his camera and called it a day, but she knew the remotes would follow her every move from here on out.

In its unfinished state, Sam's house lacked warmth and personality. The same, she thought, could be said for her boss.

And yet, if she were honest with herself, she had to admit there was more to him than she'd first believed. And that really bothered her. She didn't want to think her attraction to Sam went beyond anything more than the superficial. She could forget a handsome face and a nice build. Kyle had been attractive and physically fit. But kindness, intelligence, patience—those were qualities one didn't notice when merely infatuated.

She kicked off her heels. It was after nine. Less than three hours until she could return to her apartment and her children. Sort of like Cinderella, she mused, with an exhausted chuckle.

She'd been at a meeting that ran late. From there, she had rushed to a cocktail party given by the mayor, rubbing shoulders with Chicago's corporate class, who were mostly male. She tried not to let on that she was watching the clock.

She'd introduced herself as Sam's fill-in for the evening, leaving out the more salient details. Explaining the camera crew had required a little more creativity, but she'd stuck with the story Sylvia had concocted: a PBS station was making a documentary of women moving up the corporate ladder. If only that were true, she thought ruefully.

The telephone rang, giving her a start. She dropped the house key and it clattered on the wooden floor in the kitchen.

She hesitated after picking up the telephone. What should she say? She settled on, "Maxwell residence."

"Hello, may I speak with Samuel, please?"

It was a woman's voice. And based on her very proper tone and the way she gave his full name, Kelli deduced the caller was Sam's mother.

"I'm sorry, he's not in right now."

"To whom am I speaking?"

Kelli hesitated another moment, wondering what Sam had told his friends and relatives about his current situation.

"This is Ms. Walters," she replied crisply. "Can I take a message?"

There was an audible sigh on the other end of the line. "So, my son has finally taken my advice and gotten some domestic help. You know, I'd much rather talk to a person than an answering machine. This is his mother. I just wanted to find out if he would be coming home for his father's birthday next month."

"I'll give him the message," Kelli said, simultaneously amused and insulted to be considered the hired help.

Still, when she hung up, she found herself pondering the woman's defeated tone. It was as if she already knew what her son's answer would be and was extending the invitation only out of courtesy, habit and...hope.

She chided herself for such foolish speculation. Samuel Maxwell's life and his problems were absolutely none of her business. She had enough on her plate without worrying about a man who'd made it clear that even though he might find her attractive, he didn't particularly find her an equal, as capable and hardworking as himself.

On the counter, Kelli spotted a bottle of merlot, tipped up in one of those interesting wire contraptions that made it look as if gravity were being defied. She decided to indulge in a glass. She didn't have to drive. The limo would see her safely home at the appointed time.

No twist-off cap on this bottle, she mused, searching through the drawers for a corkscrew.

The first sip confirmed what she had suspected. Expensive wine was indeed better than the kind she could afford. It slid down her throat, smooth and warm. She closed her eyes and smiled. She had an idea.

Self-indulgence was not a word often found in a single mother's vocabulary. Children and their needs came first, leaving little time for anything else. She'd forgotten the last time she'd taken anything longer than a quick shower, one ear listening for Chloe or Katie.

She climbed the stairs and headed to the master

suite. Sam's bedroom was luxurious if austere. He had a bed, or at least a nice mattress set covered in a cozy-looking cream-colored duvet. There was no headboard or footboard, no pictures on the walls. Even the nightstand held only a lamp, telephone and of course the remote to the television she assumed was discreetly tucked behind the doors of the armoire on the wall opposite the bed.

If Sylvia hadn't relented, Kelli might have been sleeping here. In his bed. No, no, she told herself. She would have been down the hall, in one of the house's other bedrooms. But that clarification did little to keep her mind from conjuring up an image that was far less chaste than the reality would have been. She blamed it on stress, two years of celibacy and a really good glass of wine. And even so she took another sip.

In the master bathroom, she found what she was looking for: a whirlpool tub. Surrounded by gorgeous Italian marble, it was slightly sunk into the floor. Again, her mind betrayed her. It was definitely big enough for two. She set the wineglass on the side of the tub and turned on the faucet, her movements brisk and efficient to compensate for her wayward thoughts.

Just as she shed the last of her clothing, the telephone rang. She groaned in frustration, wrapping a towel around her torso as she dashed to answer it.

"Maxwell residence."

"Hello, Kelli. It's Sam."

She pulled the towel tighter, as if he could somehow see her and then knew a moment of blinding panic that had her forgetting all about modesty.

"My girls! Is everything okay?"

"Fine, fine. Sorry to worry you." He cleared his throat. "It's just that I can't find Harvey. I've searched the apartment top to bottom and there's no sign of him."

She smothered a laugh, worry replaced by amusement as he continued.

"Katie says it's her favorite."

"A rabbit, yes."

She walked back into the bathroom with the cordless telephone and sat on the edge of the whirlpool. The water felt wonderful as she plunged her feet into the tub. They weren't used to being pressed into the torture chambers known as high heels.

"So any idea where Harvey might be? She said you'd know." He lowered his voice. "I don't think she plans to go to sleep without it."

She sipped her wine, considering letting him off the hook before discarding the notion.

"Would you consider this to be one of those glitches to your system?"

She thought she heard him swear under his breath. "Never mind. I was just trying to do the kid a favor. She seems pretty worked up."

"You don't know much about kids, do you?"

"You don't have to be a professional in child care to want to see a seven-year-old reunited with a favorite toy at bedtime,'' he snapped, sounding oddly defensive.

''It wasn't a criticism, Sam, just an observation.''

The water was too tempting and because she decided the conversation might take a little time, she slipped off the towel and eased soundlessly into the tub. Or at least she thought she had, but her hand had accidentally depressed the on button and the jets came alive in all their pulsating glory.

''What are you doing?'' he asked.

''Nothing.''

''That sounds like… Are you in my tub?'' His tone was incredulous.

She didn't even consider lying. Strategy, she decided. ''Uh-huh. And drinking a glass of your merlot.'' She swirled the deep red liquid around in the glass. ''Jealous?''

''Of the tub,'' she thought she heard him mutter.

''What was that, Sam?''

''Nothing. How is it?''

''The wine or the bath?''

Sam eyed the jelly jar of iced tea on the coffee table. Beads of condensation were already streaking down Bugs Bunny's face despite the fact that Sam had just poured the beverage before calling Kelli. He was burning up alive in her airless apartment, but the thought of a hot bath sounded mighty tempting just then.

''Either…both.''

''Of course, I'm no connoisseur of fine wines, but

this vintage is excellent and your tub… What can I say? It's heaven. I might stay in here for the next hour.''

"I've never been in that tub.''

"Never?''

"Nope. It's big enough for two.''

She made a humming sound that could have been because she was sipping wine or because she was contemplating his statement. Finally, she said, "I noticed that.''

Sam stifled a groan. Last week, if an attractive woman had made such an observation to him, he would have broken the land-speed record driving to his house. Last week, though, he hadn't been responsible for two little girls, with every step and decision he made caught on camera. And Kelli was no mere attractive woman. She was the enemy.

Still, with no small amount of regret, he switched the subject. "Getting back to Harvey, any suggestions where I might look?''

"Are you a Jimmy Stewart fan?''

"Could we stick with the current subject, please?''

"I am. *Harvey* is one of Stewart's movies. It's a classic.''

The lightbulb clicked on and Sam wanted to kick himself. "The one with the eight-foot-tall invisible rabbit that only Stewart's character can see.''

"Ah, now you're catching on. We checked the movie out of the public library last week. Katie's watched it twice already.''

"She's a Stewart fan?"

"One of the few stations our television was able to get in before the antenna died broadcast classics every Sunday morning."

"She's seven and she likes Jimmy Stewart," he said.

At seven, a kid should be into *Scooby Doo* or *The Powerpuff Girls*. But he didn't say that to Kelli. From her tone, he figured she felt guilty enough about her daughter's beyond-her-years maturity.

"She's just trying to get out of going to bed, you know," Kelli said.

"But she was crying, real tears," he argued, sure she was wrong.

Sam had watched them course down Katie's cheeks and had known a moment of panic the likes of which he had never experienced before.

"Every kid knows how to manufacture tears, Sam. They're master manipulators by the time they're Chloe's age, believe me. Now, if that's all, I really want to get back to my bath before it gets cold."

He heard the jets kick on again just before the line went dead, and he decided that Katie wasn't the only one proving adept at manipulating his emotions.

Kelli crept in at midnight, pushing the door open slowly, hoping to make its squeak less pronounced. She needn't have bothered. Sam was sitting on the couch, dressed in shorts and a T-shirt and reading an issue of *Forbes* that she'd checked out of the library at the same time she'd picked up *Harvey*. Both would have to go back in a few days to avoid a late fee. She told herself that was why she was glad Sam was up, so she could remind him of that.

"That magazine is due back at the library next Thursday. The movie and a few children's books, too. Katie can show you which ones."

He set aside the magazine.

"Well, we wouldn't want to owe the library money, too." He grimaced after he said it, as if realizing the shame she felt that so many of her bills were close to falling past due. "Sorry. That was uncalled for."

"All's fair in…war."

And yet his words seemed to signal a truce when he said, "The girls had a good night."

"You got them to bed okay, then?"

"Yes. Chloe dropped off early."

"What about Katie?"

"I let her watch *Harvey*."

When she only grinned knowingly, he said, "Well, I wanted to watch it myself. I haven't seen it in years."

"School starts in a couple weeks. You'll have to start making sure she's in bed by eight-thirty. She can be a hard one to wake up even when she gets plenty of rest."

"Kids deserve to enjoy their summers." He shrugged. "I always did."

"Oh, that reminds me. Your mother called."

He grew still, rigid almost. "Did she leave a message?"

"She wondered if you would be coming home for your father's birthday next month."

When the stony silence stretched, she added, "She thought I was the help. She said she was glad you had finally hired someone so that she could talk to a person rather than a machine when she called."

"Sorry about that."

"I didn't mind. I thought she had a point. I hate talking to machines myself. Does your family know about the show?"

He shook his head. "I didn't see the point in telling them. I don't talk to them very often."

"And from your mother's tone, you visit them even less, I gather."

He glared at her. "That's really none of your business."

"Sorry. You're right."

She reached into the oversize leather bag that doubled as a purse and briefcase and pulled out a bottle of wine.

"I thought you might like a glass. Consider it a peace offering."

He eyed the merlot, and then her, and she felt her face heat at his frank appraisal.

Finally, he said, "I'll get the glasses."

They both seemed to relax once the wine had been poured. Kelli had slipped into a pair of shorts and tank top, grateful to shed the stockings and workday attire she'd been forced to put back on after her long soak in Sam's tub.

Her new clothes were kept in the guest room closet at Sam's house, as well as most of her toiletries. She'd argued with Sylvia long and hard about the practicality of the arrangement, but the producer had been adamant. If Kelli insisted on sleeping in her apartment every night, she had to drive back to Sam's house in the morning to get ready for work, even though it made far more sense to head straight to the office from the apartment. The commute to Sam's house in the suburbs and then back to downtown Chicago tacked another hour and a half onto an already long day, but Kelli made use of the comfy confines of the limo to catch up on paperwork and reading various business publications.

"I know I probably shouldn't ask, but how much did this bottle run?"

"You shouldn't ask," he said, but there was no rebuke in his gaze, only faint amusement. "I know what your budget looks like, remember? You buy this bottle of wine and your kids will go hungry for a week."

She sighed. "I had a feeling that might be the case. Well, then, here's to *Swapping Places*. I might never know how the other half lives otherwise."

She was seated on the sofa and held out her glass for the toast. Sam, who was on the chair opposite her, leaned forward. Their glasses clinked together and they each took another sip before settling back into their rightful places.

"It was nice of you to bring this over. When I went shopping today, I didn't even have enough left over for a bottle of cheap wine."

"Well, it seemed like the least I could do since I pilfered it from your kitchen. I'll buy another to replace it." Grinning, she added, "After all, I know you can afford it."

"How are you liking my life?"

She found the endless rounds of meetings and conference calls dizzying, the mountains of paperwork daunting, and the decision-making challenging and constant.

Of course, she'd have those torturous high heels permanently affixed to her feet before telling him that. Lifting her shoulders in a negligent shrug, she said, "I haven't had to call you for help yet."

"The *Harvey* call doesn't count."

"I think it does."

"I could have handled it on my own," he grumbled. "I was just trying to be a nice guy. Katie doesn't like me much as it is."

"So, technically, it was just an effort to win over Katie," she replied.

"That's right."

"That way you'd have a better chance at succeeding in my shoes."

"It couldn't hurt."

"So, technically, the phone call counts."

He scowled and sipped his wine. "We'll see what Ryan says when we meet with him tomorrow morning."

The El rattled by outside, taking the place of their conversation.

"How can you sleep with that noise?" he muttered.

"I'm usually so tired, it doesn't even register. Besides, you get used to it."

The wine moved her mood past mellow to melancholy. "You can get used to a lot of things when you have to."

"Interesting talk from a woman who's determined to work her way up the corporate ladder."

"Yes, I want a corner office someday. That's why I'm willing to put up with this. I recognize what's really important in the long run."

"Your daughters."

"That's right. My girls are at the heart of every decision I make. They are why I take night classes to earn my master's degree."

"Okay, but I have to ask, why did you take the job in the warehouse? You have a bachelor's degree, for crying out loud. That's hardly a prerequisite for checking in inventory."

"True enough. But I wanted to work at Danbury's. And at the time I applied, my choices were rather limited. I could work in the warehouse or I could work on the floor in sales."

"You'd be good at sales. How hard can it be to

talk a woman into buying an expensive dress she doesn't really need?'' he scoffed.

She ignored his question.

"I took the job in the warehouse where the pay is steady rather than as a salesclerk. I can't afford to gamble on commissions, Sam. Nor can I afford the clothes, accessories and other things salespeople rely on to polish their images.''

"You're a very practical woman.''

For some reason that didn't seem like a compliment.

"Even if I never wind up as a CEO, at least my girls can depend on me.'' She sighed wearily. "I'll work in the warehouse until I retire if it means I'll have a reliable paycheck.''

"Some people would call that settling.''

Sam made the comment hoping to see the spark of spirit flair in her dark eyes once more. He preferred that Kelli to this tired, seemingly defeated one. He wanted to win, but he didn't want to kick a puppy to do it. Where was the pit bull he'd glimpsed so often?

"Settling? No. Surviving.'' She spoke into her wineglass, as if she couldn't face him as she made this admission. Then she glanced around the small apartment.

"I have more than a lot of people have and plenty to be grateful for. But I want so much more than this for my girls.''

Sam had been sure she would say she wanted more for herself. But he should have known better. First, last and always, Kelli thought of her children.

CHAPTER SIX

WHEN the first week ended, Kelli and Sam were in a dead heat as far as scoring went. As she'd told him, the telephone call about *Harvey* had counted, but then so had the one she'd placed to him a day later.

Kelly had figured it would, and still she'd sought his input on a presentation she would be making to the Chamber of Commerce. Good managers didn't think they knew everything, nor did they try to do everything on their own, she'd reasoned. In fact, she'd read in several news articles that women tended to employ an inclusive management style. Ryan had listened patiently, nodding during her entire explanation, right after which he'd told her the panel of judges, which included several women, had marked her down for the call.

The clock moved slowly on Friday evening. Kelli counted down the minutes until midnight, eager to be home, eager to see her children. Eager to see Sam— but only so that she could rub his face in the fact that she was proving to be a worthy competitor.

Her smile faded the moment she opened the apartment door. Sam was seated in his usual spot on the sofa, but he wasn't alone. He had his arms around a woman—a very beautiful blonde who was sitting as close to him as possible without actually being on his lap. Unless Kelli missed her guess, she'd just interrupted something private.

"Oh, how embarrassing, Sam," the woman said, pulling him closer when he started to back away. "We've been caught kissing on the sofa like a pair of teenagers."

The blonde didn't look embarrassed, though, only smug as she wiped her lipstick off Sam's cheek. The crimson smudge was gone, but Kelli got the woman's not-so-subtle message. She might as well have written M-I-N-E in indelible ink across his forehead.

"I didn't realize you had company," Kelli said stiffly, addressing Sam.

He motioned toward the blonde. "This is Celine Matherly. She stopped by after the girls went to bed."

"And you must be Kelli Walters. Sam has filled me in on the…situation between you two. I hope you don't mind my popping in for a visit like this. It's just that I haven't seen Sam all week."

Celine massaged Sam's thigh with her hand, her fingertips flirting with the hem of his shorts and leaving little doubt as to the extent of their relationship. Kelli couldn't have said why it was that she felt betrayed, but she did. He hadn't lied to her. The subject of significant others had never come up. And why would it? She and Sam weren't dating. They were competing. Still, she couldn't dismiss the disappointment she felt, or the fact that Sam's expression held something suspiciously akin to guilt. She remembered that look well from the final year of her marriage to Kyle.

"Well, I'm going to call it a night," Kelli said. "It was nice to meet you, Celine. Good night, Sam."

A moment later, even with her bedroom door shut, she could hear the woman's throaty laughter.

"Well, I feel much better now that I've seen her," Celine said.

Kelli glanced at her reflection in the mirror that hung on the wall. She'd felt young and even pretty again for the past several days. Now she just felt tired and, for some reason, sad.

It was well past two when Celine left. Kelli knew this, because she'd lain awake in her bed, listening to the low murmur of their conversation and calling herself a dozen kinds of fool.

"It's pancake day! It's pancake day!" Katie hollered, dancing on the mattress around Kelli's prone form.

Kelli opened one eyelid, noted the time—seven-twenty—and groaned. She'd hoped for another hour of sleep, especially since she didn't have to rush out the door. In fact, there would be no rushing anywhere this weekend, she decided, pulling the pillow over her head.

"Come on, Katie. Let your mother sleep."

The deep male voice had her pulling the pillow off. Sam stood in the doorway, looking as tired as Kelli felt. And, well he should, she thought bitterly. She knew *exactly* how many hours of sleep he'd gotten.

"But it's pancake day," Katie argued. "We always have pancakes on Saturday mornings. Mom makes them from scratch."

"I'll be up in a minute," she mumbled.

"No need. I've got KP duty, remember? You're just along for the ride on weekends."

"No. My mom has to make them," Katie whined. "She knows how."

"I think I can figure it out, kiddo. Why don't you go get the ingredients out for me."

Katie did as he asked, complaining on her way out the door. When she was gone, their gazes connected—collided really. Just for a moment, Kelli wondered what it would be like to be a real family, to have a father for her girls, a helpmate for herself…a lover.

The thought made her angry. How foolish could she be? Had she learned nothing from Kyle? Had she learned nothing from last night?

She didn't need a man. She didn't need to hear promises that would turn out to be empty or words of love that would fail to have the backing of actions. And her girls certainly didn't need the disappointment and disillusionment of thinking they mattered to someone only to find out they could be as disposable as paper cups.

"So, you want some pancakes?" he asked.

"What I want," she said in a surly tone, "is some sleep. I didn't get much last night thanks to you and Celine."

"I'll apologize, then. We tried to be quiet."

"I don't like the fact that you're entertaining women in my apartment when my girls are home. What if they had woken up and wandered out to the living room?"

"They would have seen two adults sitting on the couch, talking."

"Talking." She sent him a bland look. "I wasn't born yesterday."

"Well, you're acting like it."

"Close the door on your way out." She rolled over, presenting him with her back.

"Gladly."

She lay in bed for the better part of the next hour, listening as Katie gave Sam instructions on everything from how to mix the batter to how to flip the pancakes. Kelli waited for him to chastise Katie, but he never did. Sam remained patient, even seeking her input. For a man who apparently wasn't used to being around children, he was a natural.

And Kelli wanted to hate him for it. She wanted to, but she found it impossible to hold his way with kids against him.

Chloe was now awake as well. Kelli could hear her daughter gurgling with laughter and banging something, probably an empty plate, on the high chair tray.

Kelli decided she might as well get up. Lying in bed past eight o'clock wasn't nearly as relaxing as she'd thought it would be, especially with her ears straining to hear every word being spoken in the kitchen.

She had just stepped out of the shower when she heard the crash, followed by the sound of crying. She tucked a towel around her torso and was out the door like a shot, dripping water as she went.

"What happened?"

Sam was holding Chloe.

"Houdini, here, got out of her high chair and managed to snag my coffee cup off the table." He jiggled the toddler on his hip. "Lucky for her, the contents were cold. It just scared her is all."

"Lucky for you," Kelli corrected. "You have to watch her every second, Sam. You can't turn your back. What if the mug had broken or the coffee had been hot?"

"It didn't and it wasn't," he said, setting Chloe down so he could mop up the mess with a dishcloth. Wringing it into the sink, he added, "I suppose she never gets into anything on your watch."

"We're not talking about me."

"And isn't that convenient."

"What's that supposed to mean?"

"You're the one who woke up this morning with a bug up her..." He glanced at the children, who were both watching them with rapt attention, and amended his original word choice to "backside."

"A lack of sleep always makes me cranky."

"I think this is about more than a lack of sleep."

So, he wanted to have it out here and now? Fine, Kelli decided.

"Katie, take your sister into the bedroom and get her dressed, please. Sam and I have something to discuss."

"Sounds like a fight to me," Katie muttered, but she took Chloe by the hand and led her out of the kitchen.

"All right, let's hear it," Sam invited.

Kelli glanced at the video camera mounted on the kitchen wall and then at the clock. Joe and his camera crew would be there by nine, which was just fifteen minutes away. Well, that left plenty of time to give Sam a good piece of her mind, she decided. But she didn't plan to do it on videotape for half the world to see.

"This way," she said, marching from the room.

There were only two places to escape the camera's notice in Kelli's minuscule apartment: the bathroom and her bedroom. She opted for the former, pulling him into the small room and closing the door tightly behind them. If she'd hoped to avoid the intimacy the bedroom posed, she'd failed miserably. Too late, she realized, she was standing in front of him wearing nothing but a towel, her discarded pajamas and panties in a heap at her feet on the floor.

Sam seemed to realize it, too. Awareness replaced the belligerence she'd seen in his eyes, and he swallowed hard before saying, "Let's just forget it."

"No," she replied stubbornly, if only to prove to

herself that she could be mature and rational even while wearing a towel, even while standing in a small, humid space with an attractive man. Her voice was a tight whisper when she added, ''I think we need to understand one another.''

Sam willed his gaze to stay above her collarbone. Kelli Walters was the most hardheaded woman he'd ever met, but that didn't obliterate the fact that her slender form did things for terry cloth that had his imagination working in overdrive.

''Fine. Spell it out,'' he replied, working to sound nonchalant, even as he inwardly sighed. God, this was going to be a long weekend.

''I don't think I'm asking too much to request that you refrain from entertaining members of the opposite sex in my apartment for the duration of the show.''

She said it so primly that he was almost able to forget she was standing before him half-naked.

''Don't you ever entertain members of the opposite sex?''

He stepped closer as he said it.

''That's not really relevant.''

''I beg to differ. We're swapping lives, remember? I do what you do. Don't you ever have any fun?''

''Define fun.''

Man, she was sexy as hell when she was acting all self-righteous. So, he stepped closer still. He wasn't sure what made him do it, but he hooked a finger down the front of her towel and yanked her forward until the only thing separating them was terry cloth…and his fertile imagination.

"You know," he said, trailing soft kisses across her cheek. Into her ear, he whispered. "Fun."

He pulled back enough to watch her eyes widen. Their breath mingled for a moment before his mouth captured hers. He felt her hands brush over his shoulders, her fingers weave into his hair, fisting there as if she never intended to let him go.

And it was at just that point that Sam felt the towel hit his feet.

Modesty would prevent her from pushing him away now, he realized, and he decided to use that to his advantage. He let his hands skim over the soft, seemingly endless skin of her back and sides, settling on the subtle flair of her hips.

"W-what are you doing?" Kelli whispered.

Sam didn't reply. He wasn't sure himself. He wanted more. More of this, certainly, but there was something else he longed for. Something far more elusive that had beckoned him since he'd first met Kelli Walters.

He pushed it from his mind and kissed her again, letting instinct and passion take him where they would. When this kiss ended, he had Kelli backed up against the cool ceramic of the pedestal sink. He was reaching up to pull off his shirt when he heard the doorbell ring.

Sam muttered an oath and closed his eyes. How could he have forgotten where he was? Or who he was with? He was supposed to be competing against Kelli, not trying to seduce her. No woman, not even his ex-fiancée, had ever caused him to lose all sense of reality or responsibility.

A glance at Kelli told him she was as confused, surprised and aroused as he was. There was some satisfaction in that, he decided, as she shoved him back a step before bending down to retrieve her towel. When she stood, she turned her back to him, pulling the towel into place. A gentleman wouldn't have watched her in the mirror above the sink, but Sam couldn't help himself. Perfection, he thought. She was pure perfection.

Her cheeks were flushed when her gaze met his in the mirror. "What...why?"

He didn't have answers, not for himself and certainly not for her. So, he kept his tone light when he said, "Just defining fun for you."

"Is it all just a game to you?" she whispered hoarsely. "Everything? Even...this?"

"What else could it be?" The response sounded flip, although he was feeling anything but. He wasn't ready to explore these emotions. He wasn't ready to admit they existed.

"Forget I asked."

They stayed away from one another for the better part of the morning, crossing paths only when necessary. By lunchtime, the small apartment was oven-hot, but the atmosphere was downright chilly.

"Can we go to the park, Mom?" Katie asked.

Kelli was seated at the kitchen table, reading over last quarter's earnings report. She had a meeting with Stephen Danbury on Monday morning and she wanted to be as prepared as possible when she met the man.

"That's up to Sam."

"Aw, Mom, come on. He's still doing laundry. It could take all day for him to finish." She offered an exaggerated sigh.

"There are only three loads, and it's not as if he's doing them by hand. I'm sure he'll finish before it's dark outside," Kelli replied dryly. "Besides, Chloe's still napping."

She heard the apartment door open and knew Sam and Joe had returned from the building's laundry room, which was located in the basement.

"Why don't you go help him fold the clothes?" When Katie opened her mouth to protest, Kelli reminded her, "The faster he finishes the sooner you'll be playing in the park."

Katie shuffled out of the kitchen and a moment later Kelli heard her say, "You're doing it wrong."

"There's a wrong way to fold towels?"

"We don't fold them. We roll them. Like this."

Kelli peaked around the corner into the living room in time to watch Katie show Sam the technique.

"Then we put them on the shelf by the shower."

Sam glanced up and caught Kelli looking.

"Your mom pointed that shelf out to me earlier."

She felt her face heat to crimson, but managed to sound nonchalant when she said, "It saves storage space under the sink. And it adds a decorative touch."

"You're a regular Martha Stewart."

"Well, I did get the idea from her magazine."

"Did you learn any of the other, uh, techniques you used in the bathroom from magazines?"

"I don't think that's important." She glanced in Joe's direction. The cameraman looked a little baffled by the conversation.

"Oh, I don't know, I might be interested in subscribing."

"Well, that would require a whole twelve-month commitment. Somehow, I doubt you could handle a whole twelve months with the same…magazine."

"I don't know. You seem as commitment phobic as me and you managed it."

"Mom gets *Martha Stewart Living* at the library," Katie said, blissfully oblivious to the strain between the two adults. "Can we go to the park when the laundry's done? Mom said I had to ask you."

Sam wiped the sweat from his brow and knew it wasn't all the result of the balmy weather.

"That's the best idea I've heard since the pancakes."

Twenty minutes later, they were on their way to the park with Chloe in the wagon along with a blanket and a grocery bag packed with their lunch: tuna fish sandwiches on whole-wheat bread and a bunch of green grapes.

They found a spot in the shade of a maple tree and Sam spread out the blanket. Nearby, children played on the swings and slide, running around oblivious to the heat. Sam took out the large cooler jug he'd brought and filled a paper cup. Lemonade had never tasted so good.

"Joe, you want some?" he asked the cameraman.

"You know you're not supposed to talk to me," Joe reminded him.

"That's right, you're invisible. So, you want some or not?"

Joe grinned from behind the camera. "Make mine a double."

They ate their sandwiches, or at least three of them did. Chloe turned up her nose at the tuna, as any self-respecting toddler would. Kelli flashed Sam a triumphant smile.

"I told you she wouldn't eat it. So much for your theory that kids wouldn't be picky eaters if their parents didn't let them get away with it. What are you going to do now, Dr. Spock?"

He rummaged in the lunch bag for a minute before pulling out a square of cellophane-wrapped cheese and a plastic bag full of fish-shaped crackers.

"Plan B," he said.

She nodded grudgingly. "You're learning."

And Sam had to admit, he was.

Later that afternoon, as they walked home from the park with a tuckered Katie and Chloe in the wagon,

Sam stopped by a flower vendor's cart and bought a red rose. He handed it to Kelli.

"Why'd you do that?"

"Truce? The next three weeks will go by a lot faster if we're not at each other's throats."

His answer seemed plausible, even if it wasn't exactly what a woman wanted to hear when a man was handing her a beautiful flower.

"Truce," she agreed.

"Besides, Katie said you buy a new one every week. The one in the vase right now is looking a little wilted. If you don't mind me saying so, it seems an odd bit of extravagance for a woman who makes her own chicken stock."

She brushed the silky crimson petals with her index finger.

"I suppose it does seem extravagant."

"Why, then?"

"They represent hope for the future and they remind me to slow down."

"Ah, I get it. Take time to smell the roses."

"Yes, exactly. Kids grow up so fast. Katie was just a baby and now she's seven."

"Seven and a half, Mom," Katie corrected from her seat in the back of the wagon.

"See what I mean?"

"My brother's boys are three and five."

"I didn't realize you had a brother. Is he younger, older?"

"Younger, but by barely a year. People mistook us for twins when we were kids."

"Does he live back East?"

"Yes."

"And he has two boys. You must miss seeing your family. I know I miss seeing mine. My parents live in Arizona. They moved there after my dad retired. I'm an only child."

"I miss them," Sam said, and for the first time in years, he admitted to himself that it was true.

The telephone was ringing when they walked through the apartment door.

"Walters residence," Sam said. "Ms. Walters? Yes, let me get her."

He held the telephone to his chest and spoke to Kelli. "It's Karl Boeke. I've been trying to reach him for weeks. He's the head of a line of German home appliances that I've been trying for months now to get to go exclusively with Danbury's for their U.S. distribution."

"What does he want?"

"I don't know, but don't blow this."

No pressure, Kelli thought, as she took the phone. "Hello?"

She watched Sam pace around the kitchen even as she listened to the man on the other end of the line extend her an invitation.

"Tomorrow? Um, excuse me while I check my

schedule," she said. Covering the receiver, she called to Sam, "He wants to meet me at two."

"Great!"

"At the Old Town Golf and Country Club. He wants to play a round of golf. He understands that that's how Americans often discuss business."

"Great. Tell him that's fine."

"Herr Boeke, my schedule is free. Yes, I'll meet you there. Looking forward to it."

She hung up the phone and collapsed onto a chair in the living room. "This is bad."

"What are you talking about? This is terrific. Do you know how many high-end department store chains have been wooing Boeke Appliances? And you've got an appointment with him tomorrow afternoon."

"I don't have an appointment with him, Sam. I have a golf…outing."

"So, what's the problem?"

She collapsed back onto the couch. "I don't know how to golf."

"Hell!"

"Exactly."

Chloe was asleep and Katie was watching *The Little Mermaid* when Sam began his first lesson. They both had decided that this bit of cooperation was worth the threat of being disqualified. The Boeke account was too big and important to play games with.

"Okay, you hold a club like this." He demonstrated the technique, locking the pinky of his right hand with the index finger of his left.

Kelli mimicked him, grasping a curtain rod in her hands.

"Now what?"

"When you start back on your swing, keep your left arm straight, like so. Don't bend your elbow. And keep you head down, eye on the ball and then just follow through."

"Right. Head down, eye on the ball, follow through," she repeated. She had no clue what he was talking about, but she nodded vigorously. She was going to die tomorrow. A slow painful death, and on a golf course of all places.

"Any other questions?" Sam asked.

"Are you Catholic?"

He snorted out a laugh. "Yes, why?"

"You might want to start praying to the patron saint of hopeless causes."

She slumped down on the couch with a sigh and he followed suit.

"Okay, Plan B."

She rolled her head sideways so she could look at him. "Plan B?"

He sat up and grinned engagingly.

"You wear *really* short shorts and an incredibly skimpy top, albeit one with a collar, since we are talking about the country club. Proper attire required," he said drolly. "And you let him win."

"Let him win. Hmm. That shouldn't be a problem."

"And flirt with him."

"You want me to flirt with him?"

"I don't *want* you to flirt with him, but in the absence of a golf game, I'm thinking…"

"What?"

"I'm thinking those legs of yours would make most men forget their names."

She should have been irritated by his sexist comment, but she felt a little flattered instead.

"They don't teach this in business school."

"No, I don't suppose they do. But it might be the best chance you have in lieu of a golf game."

Kelli sighed and stood. Holding the curtain rod out in front of her, she said, "Let's go through this one more time."

CHAPTER SEVEN

KELLI planned to go shopping Sunday morning while Sam and the girls were at church. She had nothing to wear while playing golf at an exclusive club, even among all of her new purchases for the television show. She told Sam as much.

"We'll come with you," he said.

"You just want to get out of going to church."

"Sure," he agreed, sending Joe a wink. The cameraman just shook his head and mouthed, "I'm not here."

"Besides, you need my help." His tone sobered. "And Danbury's needs Boeke Appliances."

She didn't argue with him. Somewhere in the past twenty-four hours, they had gone from competitors to allies. They were something more than that, as well, but Kelli didn't want to consider exactly what that might be. The possibilities were simply too scary.

"There's a nice upscale shop on Michigan Avenue that carries a women's golf line a lot of the ladies at the club wear." Sam consulted his watch. "It's probably not open till noon, but I bet the owners could be persuaded to flip the locks early. We'll start there."

"No."

"No?"

110

"I shop at Danbury's."

"Listen, I appreciate your loyalty to the store and all, but this is business."

"Exactly, which is why we will shop at Danbury's. And if Danbury's doesn't have the 'in' brands women are looking for when it comes to women's golf attire, I'm going to suggest to our buyers that they start getting them."

She had his attention. His full attention. So she pressed on. "Golf isn't just a man's game. A lot of women play golf."

When he arched an eyebrow, she said, "Just because I don't know how to play doesn't mean I don't read about it. Its popularity has skyrocketed across all segments of the population since Tiger Woods came along. But, popular or not, it's still a game that requires money, even at a municipal course.

"It's a game associated with affluence and the country club set, and yet suddenly half the people in the country want to play or at least look like they play. Other department stores have exclusive agreements with pros for endorsed products."

"We can't afford Tiger," he replied dryly.

"No, but we could carry more of the products he endorses. Or we could try to get an agreement with another pro. And that brings me to the mannequins."

"How did we move from golf to mannequins?"

"We didn't. We moved from clothes to mannequins. A very natural segue, I might add. Keep up, please."

He chuckled softly. "You're something else."

She crossed her arms over her chest. "I'm just saying that Danbury's mannequins all look like something right out of the nineteen fifties. It doesn't matter what kind of hip, trendy clothing you drape on them, they all wind up looking like June and Ward Cleaver."

He touched her cheek. A soft, simple stroke that shouldn't have made her pulse jump or her knees feel weak.

"I meant it as a compliment, Kelli."

When she said nothing, he teased, "This is where you say, 'thank you.'"

"Thank you."

An hour later, all four of them were at Danbury's accompanied by Joe and his ever-vigilant camera. The store had not opened yet. Sunday's business hours were noon till six. Being the acting vice president and CEO, Kelli had to admit, certainly had its perks. She had an entire department store at her disposal. No crowds. No lines at the registers. No waiting for a fitting room.

"Try this one, Mom," Katie said, holding out a pair of hot-pink shorts that would have made a Vegas showgirl blush.

"I don't think so."

"Aw, come on," Sam coaxed. "I wouldn't mind seeing you in that myself."

She tucked away her smile.

"Guys, this isn't a shopping expedition." Glancing

at her watch, she added, "I'm meeting Mr. Boeke at the club in less than three hours. I want to get there early so I can hit a bucket of balls."

Sam sobered at the reminder of the importance of the coming afternoon. It surprised him that he could have forgotten. He lifted Chloe off his shoulders and handed her to Kelli.

"All right. Let's get down to business."

The pickings were relatively slim since it was nearly September. Winter apparel had already been on the shelves for a couple of months. He went through the clearance racks with a critical eye. Based on some of the outfits left on the rack, Danbury's buyers needed to pick things up a notch if they hoped to pull in young, status-conscious adults. And Kelli was right about the mannequins as well. Even if they had been wearing the hot-pink shorts Katie found, they would have managed to look as if they were about to serve afternoon tea.

Finally, he stumbled across something he thought might work.

"What size are you?"

"Six." She leaned over and glanced at the price tag of the outfit he was holding. Even marked down nearly fifty percent, the price was still outrageous.

"Four," she amended.

"Did you just lose weight?"

"It's a well known fact in women's fashion that the higher the price, the smaller the size you can wear."

He shook his head. "Vanity."

"Don't knock it. It's proven to help sell clothes."

"And I thought I understood women," he muttered. "Go try this on."

He handed her a white skort that tied at one hip and a periwinkle polo. The shirt was sleeveless, but had the requisite collar. She had to admit, Sam had good taste.

When she emerged from the fitting room, the sight that greeted her brought a sigh to her lips. Sam was sitting on a mannequin base. Chloe was on his lap, content with a sippy cup of apple juice. Katie was seated next to him, head leaning against his shoulder and looking miserably bored. Pressure built in her chest. This is what she missed, what she'd never had even while married to Kyle. Ordinary moments, time spent together as a family.

It was what she still wanted, she realized, before calling herself a fool. There was nothing real about this moment. She and Sam would go their separate ways in three weeks. He would go back to his corner office with its killer view of the city and his beautiful girlfriend. She would go back to being a single mom, hopefully with half a million dollars in her bank account and a better chance at moving up the corporate ladder.

"What's wrong?" Sam asked. He set down Chloe and walked to where Kelli stood just outside the entrance to the women's fitting room.

"Nothing. It fits."

With his index finger, he raised her chin. "What is it?"

"Nerves," she lied.

"You'll do fine."

The kiss he gave her was quick and light, and afterward he seemed as surprised as she that he had done it. He turned to Joe.

"Edit that out, will ya?"

Joe offered an apologetic smile. "Can't do that, Sam. Sorry."

Chloe was asleep in her car seat and Katie was sipping a cola from the limo's minibar when they arrived at the club.

"Remember, ask for Dominick. He'll set you up with soft spike shoes and a glove, and he'll make sure you get a decent set of clubs and a bag. Danbury's has a membership here, so put it all on the account. The pro's name is Mark. He'll go over the basics with you, but don't worry about the game. It's probably a good idea to lose anyway."

"Then I shouldn't have a problem," she said dryly.

"Now would you relax? I swear. You're more nervous than I am."

He blew out a breath. "Sorry. Good luck."

When the limo pulled away from the curb, Katie said, "You kissed my mom."

"What?"

"In the store. You kissed my mom. Why did you do that?"

Sam glanced at Joe, who shook his head even before Sam could ask the question. "It stays on."

"It was just a friendly little kiss."

"Do you like her?"

He resisted the urge to squirm in his seat. "Sure, I like your mom."

He girded for the questions to come, but Katie seemed content to leave it at that. The muscles in his neck had nearly uncoiled when she asked, "Who's Celine?"

He eyed her suspiciously. "Why do you want to know?"

"I was awake when you answered the door the other night. I saw you kiss her. Is she your girlfriend?"

"It's complicated."

"Because you like my mom?"

"Well, I like your mom, but that's not...I mean that hasn't got anything to do with Celine or my relationship with her."

"Does my mom know you kiss Celine?"

"I think she's figured that out."

"Will you tell Celine that you kissed my mom?"

Sam's thoughts strayed to the kiss he and Kelli had shared in the bathroom. Thank goodness Katie hadn't been privy to that one. A chaste peck had her giving him the third degree.

"No, I don't think I'll tell her."

"Why not? Isn't that lying?"

"Are you sure you're seven?"

"And a half," Katie reminded him.

Sam sent Joe a baleful look. "I thought her mom was tough. I'm glad I'm not swapping places with this kid."

Joe just grinned from behind his camera.

"Head down, eye on the ball and follow through," Kelli repeated like a mantra as she attempted to hit one ball after another on the driving range. After an hour with the pro, she'd managed one fifty-yard hit. Unfortunately, the ball had stayed where it was and only a clump of the sod behind it had shot through the air.

"Good afternoon, *Fraulein* Walters."

She turned to find Karl Boeke standing behind her. He was younger than she'd thought. She guessed him to be around fifty, with a full head of dark hair streaked gray at the temples.

"Good afternoon."

She extended a hand and they shook.

"This is Helmut Reich and Ralph Schmidt, my attorneys."

"Pleased to meet you," she said, feeling outnumbered and out of her league. Still, she smiled with a sense of confidence she didn't feel and introduced the men to Vern and the rest of the camera crew, offering the same cover story about the documentary.

"I'm afraid my golf game is a little rusty," she told Karl as they strapped their bags onto the back of a cart.

"That's all right. A beautiful day, a beautiful woman, it is not so bad a way to spend my time."

As she turned to climb into the golf cart, she heard him say to his attorneys, *"Schoene beine."*

"Danke, Herr Boeke, but we're not here to discuss my legs. We're here to discuss your small kitchen appliance line and hammer out an exclusive agreement to sell it in the United States through Danbury's."

"You speak German?" He had the grace to blush.

"Not as well as you speak English, I'm afraid. But enough."

"Then I will apologize for my remark."

"No need." She crossed the legs he'd admired. "Let's play golf, shall we?"

Sam was waiting when she got back to the apartment. Kelli had barely closed the door before he was asking, "Well. What did he say? How did it go?"

"Don't you even want to know who won?" she teased.

"Just a wild guess, Boeke, right?"

"I'm distressed by your lack of faith in my abilities." But she laughed and admitted, "I decided just to drive the cart after the second hole. I nearly took out one of his attorneys with an errant shot and I had the camera crew diving for cover every time I hit the ball."

"And Boeke, what did he say?"

"Well, he told me I had nice legs."

"He told you that straight out?" Sam asked incredulously.

"No, he said it in German."

"You speak German?"

"Why is everyone so surprised by that?" she mused, picking up Chloe and giving her a noisy kiss. "How's my girl? Hmm? Were you and Katie good for Sam?"

"Kelli, you're killing me here. What did Boeke say?"

"Well, the lawyers will have to sort out the details, but, yes, he's agreed to let Danbury's sell his products exclusively in the United States for the next two years."

He let out a whoop of joy, and because he wanted to kiss her again—and not just in celebration, he realized—he settled on giving her arm a friendly squeeze.

"This calls for a toast. I'll break out the good jelly jar glasses and whip up some red Kool-Aid."

"I've got a better idea. Let's go out. I'm in the mood for champagne," she said.

"My budget won't even cover domestic beer, I'm afraid."

"I know. But I'm buying." She sent him a wink. "And the sky's the limit. I can afford it. At least for the next three weeks, and besides, your credit card bill won't come in until after we swap back."

They opted for a sitter since it would be nearly nine by the time they arrived at the restaurant. And, since she didn't have any of her fancy new clothes at the apartment, they chose a little Italian restaurant that was just a few blocks up the street. They walked, followed by the cameraman who had come on duty to relieve Joe. His presence ensured the conversation stayed on business and other safe topics.

As Kelli slid onto the red vinyl seat of a booth near the back of the restaurant, Sam found himself glad for the chaperone. He couldn't fault Boeke's eyesight. Kelli certainly did have a nice pair of legs. And even though he had jokingly urged Kelli to use them to her advantage, it rankled Sam that another man had been ogling those well-shaped limbs for the better part of the afternoon.

Sam opened the wine list, determined to stay focused on the celebration at hand.

"I don't see champagne on the menu, but it looks like they have a decent Chianti," he told her.

He ordered a bottle when the waitress came by—what the heck, neither one of them would be driving—and then he said, "All right, I want details."

"I still can't believe I pulled it off." She grinned, looking younger and happier than he could ever recall her looking. "He made some noise about a meeting with Fieldman's last week and how he wasn't sure he wanted to commit to Danbury's when he knew that the company was struggling financially."

"How did you convince him otherwise?"

"I played a hunch."

Her grin was infectious. "And what hunch would that be?"

"Boeke is a family enterprise. It goes back to his grandfather, who patented a coffee press and went into business with his brother. Well, Danbury's is a family enterprise as well, and I told him that Stephen Danbury wants to keep it that way. Fieldman's was family-owned, but it's now just part of a huge conglomerate that owns everything from the high-end department store chain to discount mass merchandisers that can be found in every suburban strip mall."

"Very smart thinking."

"Well, I couldn't very well hope to dazzle him with my golf game."

The waitress came with their wine and a basket of bread sticks. After she took their orders and left, Sam lifted his wineglass. "To a long and prosperous relationship with Boeke Appliances."

Their glasses clinked. In the soft light of the restaurant it was easy to forget this was business and that they were ultimately adversaries. But tonight, right this very minute, Sam saw only a beautiful, smart and sexy woman sitting across from him. And while the conversation remained far from intimate, and their every movement and word was caught on tape, he knew it had been a long time since he'd enjoyed a woman's company nearly as much.

Two hours later, they were back in Kelli's stuffy little apartment. Long after she'd bid him good-night and closed her bedroom door, Sam lay awake on the couch wondering about this woman whose life he'd been dropped into.

By the end of the second week of competition, a pattern had developed. Kelli and Sam would snipe and snarl at each other during their weekday meetings with Ryan, trying to find chinks in each other's armor. But when she returned to the apartment late each night, all weapons were put aside in favor of an amiable truce. Sometimes she brought wine. Sometimes he delighted her with a pathetic-looking dessert he and the girls had baked together.

They hadn't actually discussed calling an end to the hostilities at the stroke of midnight. It just sort of happened that way and kept happening, until fifteen minutes of conversation had become half an hour and sometimes longer. And Kelli had to admit, she looked forward to those late-night talks with Sam.

Sam looked forward to them, too.

More surprising to him, however, was that he looked forward to seeing the girls each evening when he came home from work. The apartment was small, ungodly hot and full of delightful, infectious laughter.

Chloe had been the first to thaw. And the first time she'd put her chubby arms out for him to pick her up, Sam had fallen head over heels.

He couldn't stop himself from wondering why a man would choose to walk away from all of this as Kyle had.

His conscience nudged him.

Hadn't he walked away from his brother's boys? He'd never spun his nephews in circles until they were dizzy or delighted laughter from them with a messy raspberry to the belly. Being a father and being an uncle weren't the same, of course, but it did surprise Sam to find he could no longer quite so neatly justify his absence from their lives based on the fact that his brother and his fiancée had betrayed him.

"You're quiet tonight," Kelli noted.

"Just thinking."

"Uh-oh." She sat with her bare feet tucked up underneath her in the chair, a glass of ice water in one hand.

"Can I ask you something personal?"

"I guess."

Sam sat forward on the couch, resting his elbows on his knees. "You're obviously a very bright and resourceful young woman."

"I'm liking this question so far," she teased, sipping her water.

"I'm just wondering what made you marry so young? You must have been, what, nineteen, twenty?"

"I was nineteen."

The grin was gone, he noted. He waited, not sure she would offer any more information and yet he wanted to know.

She let out a deep sigh. "I fell in love. I was just starting my freshman year of college when I met him.

He was twenty-three and a senior majoring in advertising. He swept me off my feet. We were married by the end of the school year.''

"But you stayed in college."

Her laugh held no humor. ''Yes. Kyle got an entry-level job at a small advertising firm in Chicago and we lived in married housing on the campus. He loved the college scene, even after he graduated. I realize now that he never wanted to grow up. I'm not sure why he married me. He certainly didn't want the responsibility of a wife.'' Her voice was a pained whisper, when she added, ''Or children.''

"Katie must have come along while you were still in school."

"My senior year. I had to take an extra semester, but I graduated the following December."

"With honors," he murmured.

"My life's an open book, or at least an open personnel file. You have me at a disadvantage."

"You have a question you want answered? Ask away."

"Okay," she said slowly, running a fingertip lazily around the rim of her water glass. The gesture seemed absentminded, so he doubted she was trying to be sexy or flirty. That was the thing about Kelli Walters. She didn't need to try.

"Well?" he prompted.

"I guess I'm wondering how it is that an attractive, successful man such as yourself gets to be thirty-four without a wedding band wrapped around his fourth finger. Or maybe you have been married.''

"No.''

"Ah, a very short answer, which means there's more to this story. Come on, offer up a few details, Sam. It's only fair after I bared my soul.''

She hadn't bared her soul. There was much more to her relationship with her ex-husband that Sam wanted to explore. Purely out of curiosity, of course. For example, did she still love him? That question was beginning to nag at him.

"Well?" she prompted.

"I was engaged once.''

"What happened?" she asked softly.

"She married my brother.''

"I'm sorry.''

"It was a long time ago.'' He shrugged.

"Not so long ago that it doesn't still hurt, I'm guessing. Is that why you don't go home much?''

A week ago, he would have told her to butt out. But so much had changed since then.

"Yes. I haven't been home in years, six years to be exact.''

"That must break your mother's heart,'' she murmured. "It must break all of their hearts.''

"Are you trying to make me feel bad?''

"No. There's no need. I know you well enough to know you already do.''

"So, you think you know me well?'' He offered a

crooked smile, more than happy to change the subject. "What's my favorite color?"

"Blue." When his eyes widened, she added, "You wear a lot of blue shirts."

"That's what I like about you. You pay attention to details. You're going to make a good corporate executive someday."

The compliment warmed her, but she was feeling just cocky enough to add, "Thanks, but I'm a good corporate executive right now."

CHAPTER EIGHT

"SAM, we need to talk."

He was literally up to his elbows in a dirty diaper when Katie made her adult-sounding announcement. Not for the first time since swapping lives, Sam decided he'd much rather sit through the most boring of meetings than change a baby's messy pants.

"It will have to wait a minute. I'm kind of busy here, kiddo."

She nodded and turned to leave the bedroom, but then paused in the open doorway.

"Um, Sam, my mom calls me Katie-did."

When she was gone, he grinned at Chloe. "I think your sister's starting to like me."

He joined Katie·in the living room a moment later with Chloe in tow. After setting the toddler down in front of a pile of colorful plastic blocks, he said, "So, what do you want to talk about?"

"I have a dilemma."

He wisely kept his smile in check at her use of such an adult word. She was seven—and a half— what did she know of dilemmas? But she was staring at him so intensely that he knew she wouldn't appreciate hearing his opinion.

"Well, tell me what it is and maybe I can help you solve it."

"There's this thing at school at the end of the month."

She had just started back to class a few days earlier. It surprised Sam, but perhaps it shouldn't have, to find that Kelli sent her daughter to a Catholic school. That meant she had to pay tuition. But somehow, despite her meager budget and the fact she was helping to pay off her ex-husband's staggering credit card debts, she managed to do it. He had to admit, he admired the way she could stretch a dollar.

"What kind of a thing?"

"A dance."

"Ah. And you don't know how to dance," he guessed. It appeared the two years of waltz lessons his mother had insisted he and his brother take would finally pay off.

"I know how to dance."

She looked so affronted that he had to hide his smile behind his hand.

"Well, then what's your dilemma?"

"I don't have a date," she mumbled so miserably that he didn't even think about laughing.

"I'm sure someone will ask you." Did they do that at seven? Sam wondered. "It's a month away."

And he thanked his lucky stars he would be back in his own life then. What would he say to a seven-year-old girl who hadn't been asked to a school dance?

"No, you don't understand." She slouched back onto the couch with a dramatic sigh. "It's a *Daddy*-Daughter Dance."

And she didn't have a daddy. At least not one who participated in her life or who took any responsibility for her welfare. Sam's heart ached, and once again he wondered how a man could father two children and then simply walk away.

Katie issued another deep sigh from her prone position on the couch before draping one arm over her face.

Sam sat down next to her. "So, you want to go, but you need a date?"

"Nah." She straightened, as if tugged to a sitting position by pride. Lifting her small chin in just the same way Sam had seen her mother do, she added, "I guess I don't have to go. I don't have a nice dress anyway."

All that pride, and only seven, Sam marveled. She really was her mother's daughter.

"So, you're not going to go?"

"Nah." She lifted her thin shoulders. "It's probably not that much fun anyway."

"Well, now I have a dilemma." He sighed just as she had done and then slumped back on the chair.

"What's your dilemma?"

"Well, I'd like to go to that dance, so I was going to ask you to go with me. But now you don't want to go."

"You want to go with me?"

She looked so hopeful, there was no way Sam could tease her. And he realized it wasn't only his tone that was sincere when he replied, "Yes, I do. I'd be honored to escort you to the Daddy-Daughter Dance."

She angled her head to the side and studied him in the exact way her mother had done on a number of occasions.

"Why?"

Kelli wasn't raising a fool.

"I don't have a daughter. This might be my only chance," Sam said.

"I guess I could go. For you," she said. "I've never been to a Daddy-Daughter Dance, either. And this might be my only chance. I don't have a dad, not really," she confided.

"I'm sure he misses you," Sam said, feeling the need to offer some sort of comfort.

"No, he doesn't."

"How can you be so sure?"

"I heard him tell my mom one time that he wished he'd never had kids. And when she was pregnant with Chloe, he said he didn't want another baby. Mom cried. She went in the bathroom and closed the door and ran the water, but I could hear her anyway."

Sam wanted to punch something, or rather someone. He wasn't the sort to pick a fight, but if he ever met Kyle Walters, he was going to deck the guy. What kind of man would say such a thing to the woman who was carrying his child? What kind of man—let alone father—made such callous remarks within earshot of a young, impressionable daughter?

"Adults can say some pretty stupid things when they're upset. It doesn't make them true."

Katie shrugged. "It's okay. I don't need him. Not even for a Daddy-Daughter Dance." The smile she sent him was radiant and rare, and it reeled in Sam's heart. "I've got you."

Something big and spiny lodged itself in Sam's throat. But he managed to say around it, "So, it's settled. We'll go together."

"Sure."

She hopped off the couch and was halfway to her bedroom before she turned.

"Thanks, Sam."

"You're welcome, Katie-did."

It was well after midnight, and both Sam and Kelli should have called it a night long ago. But the usual half hour or so they spent in one another's company, discussing their days, had stretched into well over an hour and neither seemed quite in a hurry to go to bed.

They were seated on the couch, heads reclining on the back cushion, feet propped up on the coffee table. Kelli had changed out of her office attire, trading a silk suit and blouse for the comfort of cotton jogging pants and a T-shirt. Sam also wore a T-shirt and the faded jeans Kelli recalled from her first visit to his home.

The weather had finally turned cooler, especially at

night. The breeze rustling the curtains was almost chilly. With her thumbnail, she scratched at the label on the beer bottle. Sam had mentioned missing having a good cold one when he watched the Cubs game. She'd obliged him by bringing home a six-pack of imported beer.

"Want another one?" he asked, as he stood and stretched.

The clock said one-twenty, and yet she heard herself say, "Why not?"

He returned from the kitchen with two long-neck brown bottles. He twisted the cap off hers before handing it to her. When Sam sat down, he tapped the neck of his bottle against the one Kelli held. "Here's to good beer."

"And to good friends."

"Is that what we are? Friends?" he asked.

"What do you want to be?"

She waited for his answer, surprised by the way her heart pounded. What did she expect him to say? What did she *want* him to say?

She wasn't sure, but she felt a pang of disappointment when he replied, "I thought we were adversaries. This is a competition, you know. One I fully intend to win."

She laughed. "You have such a rich fantasy life. But at the end of the day we're friends."

"Yeah. I wouldn't have expected it at the beginning."

"I know. I didn't like you very much."

"You're kidding," he deadpanned.

"Come on, admit it. You didn't like me much, either."

"I beg to differ. Even when I found you as annoying as hell, there was something about you that..." He let his words trail away. What was it about her?

"Go on."

"No need to feed your ego. You know you have hot legs," he said. But it was more than her legs. It was much more than what he'd seen that first day in the warehouse that had him looking forward to their late-night discussions and wishing that *Swapping Places* lasted much longer than a mere month.

Eager to change the subject, he said, "Chloe put a pea up her nose at dinner tonight."

She closed her eyes and groaned. "Please tell me you got it out."

"It took some doing, but yes."

He didn't mention the few minutes of utter panic that had ensued before the errant legume had been expelled.

"I'm only telling you this because I know Katie called you after dinner."

"She didn't tell me about the pea incident."

"Oh, so she ratted me out on the burned dinner, huh? In my defense, I think your oven is defective."

"She didn't mention dinner, either."

"Oh." He sipped his beer. Better to quit while he was ahead, he decided, falling silent.

"You know where I keep the fire extinguisher, right?"

"Very funny. So, why did she call?"

It was Kelli's turn to be quiet.

"Are you going to tell me or do I have to guess?" he teased.

"She said you offered to take her to the Daddy-Daughter Dance at school at the end of the month. *Swapping Places* will be over by then. You know that, right?"

"I know."

"Why did you agree to do it?"

"You need to ask?"

When she said nothing, he went on. "She's a great kid, Kelli. Both of them are. She pretended it was no big deal, but I could tell it was. I want to do this for her. It has nothing to do with the show."

"Thank you. I wish…"

"What?"

She wished she could protect Katie from this kind of pain. She wished that as a single parent, she could be all that her girls ever needed. And most of all, she realized, she wished Sam was more than a temporary fixture in their lives. But she couldn't tell him that. She could barely admit to herself that what she felt for him went far beyond simple attraction. She liked him, respected him. He made her laugh, something she hadn't done often in the past few years. And he was good with her children, not just because of the show, she felt certain, but because that was the kind of man Sam was: stable, patient, considerate, involved.

"Are you going to tell me what you wish?"

I wish you loved me.

She felt her face grow warm. Thank goodness she hadn't said that aloud.

"I wish the school wouldn't have the dance," she replied instead. "It's an annual thing, so it's hard to explain to Katie why she doesn't have a father in her life anymore. Not that Kyle was much of one when he was here. He rarely had time for me, let alone Katie."

"Then he doesn't have any contact with Katie or Chloe?"

"No. He hasn't spoken to Katie since he left and…he's never even seen Chloe. We separated while I was pregnant."

"I'm sorry, Kelli." He put an arm around her and offered a comforting hug.

"Me, too. It's a hard thing to explain to children. They automatically assume they did something wrong."

He hadn't planned to bring it up just then, but given the turn in their conversation, Sam decided to tell Kelli the rest of what Katie had said.

"Katie told me she once heard Kyle say that he wished he didn't have kids."

"Oh, God," Kelli groaned. "She must have been devastated. I'll have to talk to her about it. What did you say to her?"

"I just told her that in the heat of the moment, adults don't always say what they really mean."

"We don't, do we?" Kelli said softly. She felt Sam's fingers drawing lazy circles on her shoulder. "Sometimes we push away the people we've begun to care about when what we really want is to keep them close."

His fingers went still.

She stood. "Well, it's late. I think I'd better get at least a couple of hours of sleep."

"Kelli."

But she didn't let him say whatever it was he was going to say. The night had held too many revelations as it was. She needed to think.

"I'm glad you were here for her, Sam. You'll make a good father someday."

And with that, she was gone.

Sam stretched out on the couch, one hand pillowing his head, the other lazily swinging the half-empty beer bottle. Their conversation replayed in his head.

No, adults didn't always say what they meant, but Sam had a feeling Kelli had come awfully close tonight. And he wasn't sure exactly how he felt about that.

When the following day finally ended, Sam felt as if he had sprinted the entire length of a marathon. Work had been a bear. Arlene and two other people from their shift had called in sick with the stomach flu, leaving them short-staffed on a day when a huge holiday shipment had arrived. He'd trudged home late with barely enough time to slap together a few baloney sandwiches before heading out to class. And then, he'd discovered that being a CEO did not mean he knew all of the answers on the exam his professor had warned the class would count as twenty percent of their final grade. Sam hadn't studied, and he knew it would show when he got the test back. Why did they require people to learn that stuff? They'd never use half of it in the real world.

He said as much to Joe, who had only grinned and kept the camera rolling as Sam handed in his blue test booklet.

Sam was just finishing folding the last load of laundry when Kelli arrived home. She collapsed next to him on the couch with an exhausted sigh.

"Rough day?"

"I had to go to a cocktail party at the mayor's house."

"Poor baby."

She tilted her head sideways and squinted at him. "Do I detect sarcasm?"

"Not at all. I'm just finding it hard to work up much sympathy for you. Clinking glasses with Chicago's movers and shakers is hardly as taxing as…"

"Go ahead. You can say it." She poked him in the ribs. "My life is no cakewalk, is it?"

"I never said it was."

She laughed loudly before he reminded her to keep her voice down. "It took me forever to get Chloe to sleep tonight. She was still up when I got home from class.''

She kicked off her shoes and rubbed one stockinged foot.

''It's lucky for you I'm too tired to gloat.''

He took over rubbing her foot and she angled sideways until her head was against the armrest.

''What are you saying, Kelli? Are you trying to tell me that my life isn't the vacation you imagined it to be?''

She opened her mouth to protest, but then yawned. Her eyes were already sliding shut when she said, ''How about we call it a draw?''

And with that she drifted off to sleep.

Sam was too tired to carry Kelli the dozen steps it would take him to reach her bedroom. He was too sore to do the chivalrous thing and either sleep sitting in the chair or on the hard floor. And he was too exhausted to wonder what the folks at *Swapping Places* would have to say about the scene the camera would no doubt record. He reached over and switched off the lamp before sprawling out next to her. The last thing he remembered before sleep beckoned was kissing her temple and hearing her sigh his name.

CHAPTER NINE

KATIE'S bangs were still slightly crooked and instead of shoulder-length tresses, she now sported what Sam supposed an optimistic stylist might call a bob. He'd tried his best to even out the mess she'd made of her once-gorgeous mane of hair.

"Do you think my mom will notice?" the little girl asked with a mixture of apprehension and resignation.

"Well, she is pretty observant," Sam hedged.

"Maybe I could wear hats till it grows out."

"Nah." He tapped Katie on the nose with his index finger. "I think your best bet is to come clean and tell her you wanted to wear your hair like the girl in the Barbie ad, but you got a little carried away with the scissors."

"Or maybe you could tell her?"

Katie smiled, turning loose the full wattage of an adorable, gap-toothed seven-year-old. Sam shook his head and with a weary laugh admitted defeat.

"Okay. But you owe me. Big."

"I can cook dinner," she offered. "I know how to make spaghetti."

"Nah. I was thinking more along the lines of a hug."

She blinked in surprise and her smile faltered. "A hug?"

"You know, where you wrap your arms around me and squeeze. A hug." When she just stood there eyeing him suspiciously, Sam decided to add a dare. "What's the matter, Katie-did? Scared of me?"

"I'm not scared of anything."

Her tiny chin jutted out and Sam was reminded of her mother. And it occurred to him then that both Katie and her mother were afraid of him. Not physically, for surely they knew he would never raise a hand to them. But emotionally, they weren't willing to trust Sam or any man for that matter. Again, he fantasized about a nice solid jab to Kyle's jaw.

"How about a handshake? We could make a secret handshake," he offered.

"Okay."

Five minutes later he had her laughing hysterically as they choreographed an elaborate handshake.

Kelli sat through five meetings before noon. And even though she should have been concentrating on what a marketing consultant was saying about a focus group's findings on Danbury's products, her mind wandered back to that morning. She had awakened in Sam's arms, the two of them fitted together like a pair of spoons on her narrow couch. She'd felt his breath, warm and even, feather against her cheek. She'd wanted to stay there and enjoy the feeling of being safe, cherished.

His eyes had opened when she sat up.

"Guess we fell asleep," he'd murmured.

"Looks like," Kelli had replied, pushing the hair back from her face. She could only imagine what she looked like. She'd squinted at the clock that hung on the wall. "I'd better get going."

He'd placed a hand on her arm. "Kelli."

She'd covered his hand with her own and squeezed. "Time for Cinderella to turn back into the princess."

"Yeah. See you tonight."

Sam waited until the girls were occupied with a Disney video to call Celine. Their relationship was going nowhere, and it wasn't fair to her to continue it. Of course, she'd known going in that he wasn't interested in a serious commitment. He hadn't been since Leigh had shattered his life with her announcement that she loved his brother and wanted to marry him instead. Celine had told him a casual relationship was fine with her. But he knew women well enough to recognize jealousy and possessiveness. And since he'd been living in Kelli's apartment, both had become apparent.

"This is a pleasant surprise," she said into the phone. "Tired of playing Mr. Mom?"

Sam *was* tired, exhausted actually, but it surprised him to find he wasn't tired of being around Kelli's kids. There was something rejuvenating about watching Chloe discover the small pleasures he'd long taken for granted and having Katie sit close to him on the couch as he read Dr. Seuss. They still hadn't worked their way up to a hug, but Sam figured it was only a matter of time.

He turned away from Joe and, keeping his voice low, he said, "I'd like to talk to you."

"This sounds serious."

He ignored her comment. He didn't believe in conducting personal business over the telephone. And what he had to say to Celine needed to be said face-to-face.

"Do you think we could meet for a drink?"

"Are the kiddies allowed in a bar?" Her tone had turned sharp, but he chose to ignore it.

"I have class tonight, so the sitter will be here. I can ask her to come early and meet you at O'Malley's around six."

"I suppose I can break away."

From what, he wanted to ask. As far as he knew, Celine's days consisted of shopping, socializing and visits to an exclusive salon to have her nails done and hair coiffed. At one time, he'd found her lack of responsibilities amusing and convenient. It wasn't often she couldn't rearrange her schedule to accommodate his. His mother was the same way. And Leigh had been as well. Even with a degree from Vassar, his ex-fiancée had never held a paying job.

There was nothing wrong with that, but these days he found himself enamored of a different kind of woman. One with calluses on her palms. One who could read a bedtime story and a finance report with equal aplomb.

And that more than anything, he realized, was why he needed to end things with Celine.

"See you then."

Of course, when you were a single parent, even if only for a month, it quickly became clear that things rarely went according to plan. Sam thought about the conversation he'd had with Kelli in his office before their swap. Had he really thought she lacked organizational skills? Had he really thought child-rearing could be systematic?

If he had, he now knew better. Mrs. Murphy called twenty minutes before Sam was to meet Celine.

"I'm sorry, Mr. Maxwell, but I can't watch the girls tonight or probably for the next week. My mother fell and broke her hip. She's ninety and the doctors are pretty concerned. I'm flying to Florida tonight."

"I'm sorry to hear that. I hope all goes well."

"Kelli asks Miriam Davies in apartment 12B to watch the girls when I can't come. I hope she's available on such short notice."

"Thanks. And don't worry about us. We'll be fine."

He'd been less optimistic after a visit to 12B. Miriam was going out to dinner with her daughter's family that night, but at least she could watch the girls for the rest of the week.

Back in the apartment, Sam sighed and mulled his

options. It was too late to call Celine at home. She would be at O'Malley's by this point, and even if he could reach her by cell phone to reschedule, Sam didn't want to postpone this particular meeting.

He grabbed the diaper bag and with two kids in tow, headed to the El with the ever-vigilant Joe hot on their heels. The cameraman had at least compromised enough to assure Sam that his private conversation with Celine would not be recorded.

When he reached O'Malley's, he spotted Celine sipping a martini in an intimate booth toward the back. Her eyes widened briefly when she spotted him and the girls and then they narrowed into menacing slits when her gaze shifted to Joe.

"I can't believe you," she hissed, standing to leave. "I don't think we need an audience."

"It couldn't be helped. Um, you remember Joe from the other night."

"Ma'am," he said, poking out from behind the camera mounted on his shoulder.

"And this is Katie and Chloe. They were in bed when you came over to the apartment."

"Pleasure," she spat. "Now, I'm leaving. Call me when you're done playing daddy, Sam."

She stalked out of the tavern, looking like an angry goddess. Some of the men in the place looked at him like he was nuts to let someone who looked like Celine go. All Sam felt was relieved.

"That went well," Joe said.

"Yeah, I have a feeling the conversation we were supposed to have is a moot point now."

He shifted Chloe to his other hip. "Since I'm playing hooky from class tonight, what do you say we go all out and stop for ice cream on the way home?"

Chloe clapped her chubby hands in delight and squealed.

"I-cream, Da-dee."

Sam went still, even as his heart picked up speed, pounding out those two syllables in his head over and over. *Da-dee, Da-dee, Da-dee.*

"Kinda grabs you by the throat the first time you hear them say it, doesn't it?" Joe said.

Sam didn't reply. He couldn't. But he knew the cameraman was right.

They were a block from the apartment when it happened. Katie and Chloe had been quietly—if messily—consuming their ice-cream cones when Katie stopped walking. Sam knew if he lived to be a hundred he'd never forget the look of panic on the little girl's face. Her eyes grew wide even as her breathing became labored.

And sticking out from the top of her chocolate ice cream were a few tiny fragments of tan. Recognition came in a flash. Peanuts.

Sam pushed Chloe toward Joe.

"Watch Chloe and call 911," he screamed, even as he scooped up Katie and made a mad dash toward the apartment. A wide receiver, holding the ball for the winning touchdown of the Super Bowl, didn't move as fast. He burst through the door of the apartment house and didn't bother to wait for the elevator. He took the stairs two at a time, propelled by adrenaline and bone-chilling fear.

At the apartment door, he fumbled for the keys, losing precious seconds. Katie was still making wheezing sounds, which he took as a good sign, even though her face was ghostly white and her skin clammy.

"Hang in there, Katie-did, hang in there," he urged.

He laid her on the couch and rushed to the bathroom. He found the syringe in the medicine cabinet. When he reached Katie, her pupils were dilated and her skin had turned blue.

"Oh, God!" He pushed the needle into her limp arm and depressed the plunger, praying harder than he had ever prayed in his life. In the distance, he thought he heard an ambulance siren. Hurry, he silently pleaded, as he smoothed the hair back from Katie's damp face.

"Come on, Katie-did. Come on."

"Is she all right?"

Joe stood behind him, holding Chloe, who whimpered.

"I don't know."

Kelli's heart was pounding when she burst through the double doors of the emergency room.

"My daughter!" She gulped for air. "Katie Walters. She was brought here by ambulance for an allergic reaction."

The white-coated woman behind the desk calmly clicked the computer mouse. Clearly, she was used to panicked parents.

"She's being admitted, Mrs. Walters."

"Is she okay?"

"The doctor will be out in a minute to talk to you. In the meantime, I have some papers for you to fill out."

"Is she okay?" Kelli repeated, on the verge of hysteria.

The woman smiled sympathetically. "Honey, I can't tell you that. I'm just the person who works the front desk and takes the insurance information. Why don't you go wait over there with your husband? He might know more."

"Kyle?" Kelli said half to herself. But when she turned, it was Sam she spotted sitting in one of the hard-backed chairs of the crowded waiting room. His elbows were propped on his knees, his head supported by his hands. He looked to be as in need of comfort as she was, but Kelli needed answers more than anything else right now.

"Sam, what's happening? How's Katie?"

He stood and, without saying a word, wrapped her in a fierce hug that had her heart tripping in triple time.

"My God! Is she going to be okay?"

"Yes, sorry. I didn't mean to scare you. I just…" He held out a hand—a hand that shook. And yet she trusted him completely when he said, "She's going to be fine now."

Kelli closed her eyes and sagged against him. It was several minutes before they spoke.

"What happened? The message Lottie got to me at the benefit I was attending was pretty cryptic."

"There were peanuts mixed in with her ice cream. It happened so fast. One minute she was fine. The next… My God, she couldn't breathe."

Kelli understood his horror. She'd experienced it herself once before. And she knew from the doctors she'd spoken with that allergic reactions such as Katie's would only get more severe each time she was exposed to peanuts.

"But you gave her the shot."

"Yeah. I did it just like you said."

He'd saved her child. She kissed his cheek and then his lips, simple kisses made potent by the emotions she was feeling.

"Thank you, Sam."

They sat down to wait for the doctor. Joe was there, Kelli realized, holding Chloe, who was fast asleep. His daughter Nic held the camera. The ever-vigilant camera. And even so, Kelli left her hand tucked inside Sam's when they sat. The link was like a lifeline. Somehow, in the midst of utter chaos, Kelli had found peace.

*　　*　　*

It was late when they returned to the apartment. Katie was to spend the night in the hospital. After the doctor assured Kelli that her daughter was going to be fine and probably wouldn't awaken till morning thanks to the sedative she'd been given, Kelli finally had agreed to go home.

Chloe barely stirred when Sam laid her in the crib. Standing beside him, Kelli remarked, "Children look like angels when they sleep. I still creep in every night to check on the girls and watch them when they are finally still. Whenever I start wondering what the point of it all is, I just have to look at my girls to know. They're the point, Sam. They're the one remarkable thing I've managed in an otherwise unremarkable life."

Her voice broke off on a sob.

Sam put his arm around her and pulled her into his embrace. "Katie's going to be fine, Kel. We'll go get her in the morning and you'll see. She'll be running around here, back to her sassy self by tomorrow night."

"I hope so."

They walked back to the living room and settled onto the couch.

"I can't thank you enough for what you did today. You saved her life."

"And took ten years off my own in the process. I've never been that scared," he admitted.

It was her turn to offer a hug.

They were quiet for a long time, listening to the

rhythm of the city outside the window, the click-clacking of the elevated train accompanied by a medley of car horns and sirens and barking dogs.

"I've decided to go home for my father's birthday," Sam said.

"Your mother will be pleased, I'm sure. What made you decide?"

"Today, tonight. Katie."

He thought about his nephews. The sons he had long begrudged his brother and ex-fiancée.

"I've never met my brother's boys. I was so busy being angry at Donovan and Leigh that I didn't realize what I was missing."

He laughed harshly.

"All this time I felt guilty because I hadn't been a part of their lives. I felt guilty, thinking about what *I* was depriving *them* of with my absence. Talk about hubris. I never stopped to consider that I was depriving myself as well."

"Family is everything, Sam."

"I know." He raised her hand to his lips and kissed the back of it. "Thank you for reminding me."

Kelli took the day off from work to spend with Katie. The show had agreed to give her twenty-four hours without cameras. Sam was given the day off as well. He decided to go back to his house and give Kelli some privacy, even though he found he wanted nothing more than to spend the day with her, Katie and Chloe.

His house was big and quiet when he let himself in through the front door after the limo dropped him off. If it had lacked the feeling of home before, it seemed even more sterile to Sam now without a toddler's squeals and a little girl's questions to distract him. He turned the corner into the great room and tripped over an ottoman. While they had been living one another's lives, Kelli had been meeting with his decorator. She'd been mum on the result, other than to tell him she thought he would like it.

He glanced around the great room and nodded in appreciation. He wouldn't have gone with the crimson couch with its floral pillows, but he had to admit, it looked fantastic and it brought out the colors in the large painting that hung on the wall and the richly patterned area rug that filled the center of the room. Other furniture was grouped around it into a conversation area that made the large room seem cozy. Kelli had a way of making things comfortable, homey.

Upstairs, he sat on the edge of his bed, listening to the silence. Why was it that even though he hadn't had a day free of obligations in months, the next twenty-four hours stretched out before him long and lonely?

Kelli's words came back to him. *Family is everything.*

He picked up the telephone and dialed the familiar number. His mother answered on the second ring, and he pictured her sitting in her favorite chair by the fireplace maybe working on some cross-stitch or reading a book.

"Hi, Mom, it's Sam."

"Sam! Oh, it's so good to hear your voice." He recognized both heartache and joy in her tone and he knew he was the source of both.

"Yeah. It's good to hear your voice, too."

"Everything's okay there in Chicago?"

Of course she would think something was wrong. He knew a moment of self-loathing that a simple phone call home would spark concern.

"Everything's fine, Mom. I just called to say that I'll be coming home…for Dad's birthday."

"That's wonderful! Your father will be so pleased." She hesitated a moment before adding, "Donovan will be here. And Leigh."

"And the boys, too, I'm hoping. I think it's time I met my nephews."

"Oh, Sam."

"I'm thinking about bringing someone. A few someones, actually. I've met a woman." A simple statement that didn't begin to describe the cataclysmic event that had taken place in his life during the past few weeks.

His mother said nothing.

"Mom, are you still there?"

"I'm here." Her voice wobbled.

It was his turn to ask, "Is everything okay?"

"Perfect, Sam. Everything's just perfect now."

And Sam had to agree.

CHAPTER TEN

SAM knocked around his big, quiet house for the better part of the afternoon before he finally gave up pretending there wasn't someplace else he'd rather be. He just wanted to check on Katie, he told himself, even as he shaved for the second time that day and slapped on some cologne. He was humming when he climbed into the driver's seat of his car. It took him a moment to recognize the tune. Then he laughed aloud. It was the theme song to Disney's *Beauty and the Beast*.

It was five o'clock and Kelli had hovered over Katie for the most of the day, even though her daughter was hardly in need of such vigilance. But Kelli couldn't help it.

What if…? The possibilities haunted her. She'd meant it when she told Sam he'd saved Katie's life. Looking at her daughter now, all pink and grinning as she played with her dolls, it was hard to believe she had come close to dying just twenty-four hours earlier.

"Can we have pizza for dinner?" Katie asked.

Kelli knew it wasn't really in the budget, but she felt like splurging.

"Pepperoni and green pepper?"

"Pepperoni and extra cheese," Katie bargained.

"Okay." Kelli gave in knowing neither of her girls would eat green pepper anyway.

When the bell rang thirty minutes later, Kelli opened the door with a twenty-dollar bill in her hand. Sam stood on the other side of the threshold, looking far more appetizing than a Chicago deep-dish pizza.

One corner of his mouth lifted into a lazy smile that shouldn't have caused her pulse to rev, but it did.

"No need to pay me. This visit is strictly pro bono."

"What are you doing here?" Kelli asked, not quite able to keep her own smile in check.

"Sam!" Katie cried, launching herself at him before wrapping her arms tightly around his waist.

Sam was grateful for the reprieve from answering Kelli's question. Things needed to be said, but he wasn't sure right now was the best time. He got down on one knee, surprised by the usually reserved child's show of affection—and elated by it.

"Hey, Katie-did. How are you?"

She shrugged nonchalantly. "I'm okay."

"You scared the life out of me and you're just okay?" He reached out and tickled a laugh from her. Then he pulled her close.

"You feel better than okay to me."

"I love you, Sam," the little girl said solemnly.

His gaze connected with Kelli's. Her eyes were bright with tears. Sam knew that Katie's words were spoken from the heart and hearing them did funny things to his own.

"And I love you."

All, he added silently, accepting at last that even though he'd carefully dodged anything even remotely akin to that dangerous emotion for the past six years, he'd fallen hard for not one, but three females in the space of mere weeks.

They had eaten pizza and brought the television and VCR out into the living room to watch videos that Sam had rented from the corner video store. Chloe nodded off during the second half of *The Lion King* even as Katie began yawning. When her eyes finally closed, Kelli and Sam carried the girls to their room.

"Oh, to be seven again," Kelli said on a sigh. "Last night she was in the hospital, and today she had more energy than I do after a pot of coffee."

"Kids are pretty resilient," Sam said with a nod.

"Yeah."

"Are you up for some popcorn? Maybe another movie?"

"I could be persuaded," Kelli replied. "What's the other movie?"

"*Die Another Day.* Arlene mentioned that you had a weakness for James Bond."

"I'll bet she did."

A couple of hours later, after James Bond had saved the free world from disaster and made love to a beautiful woman or two, Kelli and Sam sat on the couch in the dimly lit living room.

"By the way, are you going to tell me about Katie's new hairdo?"

He rubbed a hand over the back of his neck. "Noticed that, did you?"

"Kind of hard not to."

"Yeah, well Katie wanted to wear hats for a few weeks until it grew out, but I talked her into coming clean." He shrugged. "Actually, she talked *me* into coming clean for her."

"So?"

"Well, there was this Barbie ad in the newspaper," he began. "And the little girl in it—'"

"She wants a Barbie," Kelli interrupted.

"Christmas is not far off."

"She doesn't *just* want a Barbie, she wants Ken and the entire Dreamhouse. She wants a family," Kelli whispered. "I can't give her one of those."

"Are you sure?"

He pulled her forward for a kiss, and even as he told himself to keep it light, he heard her sigh and knew he was doomed. They had somehow managed to keep things neutral between them since that day a couple of weeks earlier when her towel had slipped and passion had overridden sanity. But nothing could hold back the need now. It tangled with desire so hot that Sam was surprised the apartment's sprinkler system didn't go off.

"I've wanted to do this for a long time," he whispered, shifting their positions so that they were reclining on the couch. "Since that day in the warehouse when I spotted you wearing those snug jeans, I've had these fantasies."

"We can't do this," she said, even as she pulled him toward her for another kiss.

"It's crazy, I know. We should stop." His fingers inched beneath the hem of her T-shirt, making a mockery of his words.

Kelli stopped his hands. "What about Celine?"

"There's no Celine. Not anymore. I broke it off with her the other day."

"Why?"

His laugh was strangled. "I'm laying on top of you and you have to ask?"

"I'm not one to play at romance, Sam," she said seriously. "And I'm not into casual sex. I've got too many responsibilities for that."

He didn't know whether to kiss her or kill her. Could she really think, even now, that a quick tumble was all he was after?

"I'm not interested in playing at romance, either. As for what's been happening between us, and what *will* happen in the future," he stressed, "it goes far beyond casual. This is more than hormones. This is more than chemistry. I think it could be much more. Do I need to spell it out for you?"

Kelli wasn't one to act coy, so she wasn't playing a game when she replied, "I wish you would."

"I—"

"Ma-ma. Ma-ma." Chloe's cries interrupted what Kelli had hoped was going to be a declaration of love.

She offered an apologetic smile.

"That kid has lousy timing," Sam whispered, resting his forehead against hers for a moment. Then he rolled off of Kelli and stood up, holding out a hand to help her to her feet.

"I'll just be a minute," she promised.

He pulled her into his arms as she tried to brush past him. "Take your time. My feelings aren't going to change."

As Sam watched her walk down the hallway, he caught sight of the remote camera mounted on the living room wall. The red light winked at him. Was that thing on?

He consulted his watch. It was twenty minutes after midnight. It appeared their day off the record was officially over. Sam wondered exactly what had been caught *on the record* when the camera had blinked back to life.

"What's wrong?" Kelli asked when she returned to the living room a couple of minutes later.

"It appears the cameras are recording once more."

Her eyes grew wide as she gazed first at the unblinking lens and then at the couch.

"You don't think…?"

"It's hard to say."

Even dying of mortification, Kelli tried to find a bright side. "Thank goodness we didn't get too carried away."

"Don't worry. I'm sure they won't use any of that footage," Sam said.

"What do you think Ryan will say? We weren't exactly acting like adversaries," Kelli noted.

"Guess we'll find out tomorrow," Sam replied.

It wasn't their status on the television show that bothered him as much as the realization that the moment was ruined. Neither of them would feel comfortable discussing their relationship or the future with the camera rolling or with the possibility of another interruption from the children.

It could wait, he decided. He wanted it to be perfect anyway.

"I think I'd better go. Walk me to the door?"

She complied. Once she'd unbolted the locks, he tugged her into the hallway and closed the door behind them. His kiss was quick but lethal, leaving her limbs weak and her breathing labored.

"Think of me tonight."

When he was gone, Kelli slipped back into her apartment, turned out the lights and pulled on one of Sam's T-shirts in place of pajamas.

Drifting off to sleep, she did as he requested.

Kelli felt as if she were in the principal's office when she showed up for the luncheon meeting with Ryan the following day. Sylvia was there, stalking around the room in spiky heels and a steel-gray suit and looking none too pleased. At the other end of the conference table a team of dour-looking lawyers rifled through papers.

"I'm not very happy," Sylvia began needlessly. It wasn't as if it required psychic abilities to figure out something was wrong.

"The show overlooked the fact that you two became collaborators rather than competitors when it came to the golf outing with the Boeke Appliances' CEO," Sylvia intoned in her gravelly voice. "We overlooked the fact that the pair of you seemed awfully cozy on more than a couple of occasions. Actually, a few of our production people thought that was kind of cute and even had an office pool going on when the pair of you were going to hook up. But last night can't be overlooked."

She pressed the button on her laptop computer and angled it so Kelli and Sam could see the screen.

Kelli nearly choked on her tuna salad as she watched her and Sam writhe around on the sofa. She wanted to die.

"That won't be aired on television, will it?" Sam asked. He didn't look mortified, he looked angry.

Sylvia arched one eyebrow. "Hardly. In fact, none of it will. I think we spelled out the rules of the contest pretty clearly in the packet of information we gave you. You both signed statements saying you agreed to abide by them. You didn't. You're disqualified."

"Both of us?" Kelli asked.

"I don't believe I saw you putting up much of a

fight, Ms. Walters,'' Sylvia replied. ''Our lawyers have some papers for you to sign.''

''Danbury's attorneys will want to look at those.''

''Fine. I'm sure they'll agree they're airtight and absolve the show from any liability.''

He gave a curt nod and stood. ''This meeting is over then.''

Sylvia stalked out, followed by the lawyers.

''Sorry about this,'' Ryan said, offering a handshake. With his chin, he motioned in Kelli's direction. ''And good luck.''

So, this was it, Kelli thought. Cinderella's ball was officially over.

''I needed that money,'' she said quietly as they stood in the empty conference room. ''And if I didn't win, I needed the exposure. I've taken a semester off from classes.''

''I'm sorry.''

''It's not your fault, Sam.'' She smiled sheepishly. ''Here I am complaining, when you're in the same boat. Danbury's could have used the national exposure.''

''I don't regret it. Any of it. Do you?''

''No.''

He glanced at his watch. ''I'd better get back to work.''

''Which job?'' Kelli asked.

''The one I started today. I believe in finishing

what I start," he said, drawing her by the hand. They walked in companionable silence to the elevator.

"Let's go out to dinner tonight. My treat since our lives and bank accounts are our own once again." He squeezed her hand, and then raised it to his lips for a kiss.

A bell sounded and the down arrow lit up. Sam stepped inside the elevator. "I think we've got some things to discuss."

The doors slid shut, and Kelli turned, nearly running straight into Celine Matherly.

"Pardon me."

Celine said nothing, but her pinched gaze traveled up and down Kelli's length before returning to her face. Kelli had no doubt she'd just been measured in full—and found supremely lacking. The woman's expression all but screamed: he prefers this to me?

But then she offered a pleasant, almost friendly smile.

"It's Kelli, isn't it?"

"Yes," she replied, wary of the woman's sudden shift in attitude.

"I was just here dropping some things off of Sam's. I hope you don't mind. I left them in his— your—office." She giggled almost girlishly, but it seemed forced.

"That's fine."

"I suppose Sam told you our relationship is over. Did he tell you why?"

"It's really none of my business."

When Kelli would have stepped past her, Celine laid a hand on her arm.

"Come now, woman to woman, let's be honest. There's something going on between the two of you."

"That would be none of *your* business."

"Perhaps." Celine shrugged delicately, but continued. "I wasn't intentionally eavesdropping just now, but I did hear part of your conversation. I just thought I should warn you that Sam comes on strong at first, but it doesn't last."

"No offense, but I don't see what concern that is of yours," Kelli replied pointedly.

"You're right, it's none of my business. It's just that…oh, forget it. I'm sure his…track record in other cities wouldn't matter to you. When I heard about it, it bothered me. In fact, I was just about ready to end things between us when he did. There's certain behavior that can't be overlooked, even with someone as handsome and well off as Sam."

Celine started to walk away and even though Kelli knew she was being baited, she heard herself ask, "What is it you're dying to tell me?"

"I've heard a rumor that this sort of thing has happened before at other stores in the Danbury chain where Sam worked."

"Celine, this isn't high school. Why don't you quit being coy and just spit it out? I've got work to do."

Celine's eyes narrowed to little slits, but her tone remained pleasant.

"You're not the first. He's had relationships with *underlings* in the past. They've all been quietly…settled."

Kelli didn't care to be reduced to an underling, but she had to admit her curiosity was piqued, but she said only, "Sam's past is his business."

"Well, that might be true, but you might want to consider that Danbury's does have a no-fraternization policy. Add to that sexual harassment."

"Sexual harassment! What are you insinuating?"

"Just that you could have him fired. He's management after all. Even dating one's inferior can constitute sexual harassment if it creates—what's the term?—oh, yes, a hostile work environment." She stepped closer to Kelli, bringing with her the cloying scent of her perfume. "This is just a little friendly advice—woman to woman. Get yourself a good lawyer and you won't need to work ever again."

"But I'm the boss in this case," Kelli replied, too shocked by the woman's scheming to offer the stinging rebuke it deserved.

"The boss?" Celine laughed outright. No girlish giggling this time. "Only in Hollywood. If you're smart, and I think you are, you'll take my advice. When this so-called reality ends, so will the romance. You have two girls. Make sure you get something out of this experience. What the show's offering if you win is peanuts compared to what a good lawyer could get for you. Danbury's has deep pockets. Think about it."

Her feline smile lingered as the door slid shut.

Obviously, Celine wasn't privy to the fact that Kelli and Sam had been disqualified or she probably would have used that in her argument. What a spiteful and vindictive woman. Her physical beauty notwithstanding, Kelli had to wonder what Sam had ever seen in her.

When she turned, she ran into Lottie Branch. The woman eyed her coolly.

"Mr. Boeke is on the line. I didn't think you'd want to miss his call."

"Thanks, Lottie," she replied with a smile.

But the older woman's expression remained reserved. No doubt she'd overheard the conversation. But, Kelli didn't have the time—or the inclination—to explain the matter to her. What went on between her and Sam was no one else's business. Not Lottie's and certainly not Celine Matherly's.

Chin raised, she went to take the phone call.

"I normally don't repeat private conversations or things I overhear. But I thought you should know, Mr. Maxwell."

Sam smiled at Lottie Branch. She'd been a loyal employee to Danbury's for years, and even though she had only known Sam for a matter of months, apparently she was willing to extend that loyalty to him.

Still, he didn't want to believe her.

"I appreciate you telling me this, Lottie. But you

must have misunderstood. Kelli Walters isn't the type to claim sexual harassment.''

''No offense, Mr. Maxwell, but when money is involved, people will do and say all sorts of things that might otherwise seem out of character. I'm just telling you what I heard Ms. Walters and Miss Matherly discussing.''

After Lottie left, Sam sat in the small break room and considered her words. If the information had come from someone like Celine, he would have dismissed it out of hand. But Lottie Branch had no ax to grind, no score to even. So, the words carried a weight they otherwise would not have.

Could Kelli be considering a lawsuit? Being disqualified from the show had left her disappointed. He remembered her fallen expression as they'd stood in the conference room.

I needed that money, she'd said. Would she now consider going for an even bigger payout?

With a groan, Sam realized that the kiss that was caught on camera would provide wonderful documentation of Kelli's case, should she decide to take this matter to court. She'd kissed him back, but would that matter?

At the very least, she would have proof enough to have Sam removed from the company based on Danbury's no-fraternization policy. Maybe she planned a little blackmail, her silence for an ample settlement.

I'd do anything for my girls. How many times had

she told him that? Did that include perjuring herself and destroying his career?

No, he didn't believe it. He wouldn't. Sam considered himself a good judge of character, and he didn't believe Kelli was the type to cheat or scheme to get her way. But then he remembered Leigh. His trust in her had been sorely misplaced. His fiancée and his brother had been carrying on a full-fledged romance right under his nose and he'd never suspected a thing until she'd handed back the ring just months before the wedding.

He pushed aside the old bitterness. *I'll talk to Kelli*, he decided. *I'll give her a chance to explain.*

And yet he struggled with doubt for the remainder of his shift.

"You've certainly been quiet today," Arlene commented as they punched out.

Sam shrugged. "A lot on my mind."

"I'll bet." She grinned. "And I think I know who she is."

"What do you mean?"

"All I know is that if you looked at me the way you looked at Kelli the last time she was in here, I'd be hauling you before a judge. It's criminal."

She winked after she said it. And even though he knew she meant it in jest, he felt compelled to point out, "I've done nothing inappropriate."

"Aw, come on now. Don't ruin my fantasy," Arlene complained. "I was hoping that girl was having a little fun with the boss."

CHAPTER ELEVEN

KELLI spent the remainder of the afternoon tidying up Sam's office and trying to get through the paperwork stacked up in the in-box. Lottie had left right after lunch, saying something about a dental appointment she'd forgotten to mention.

It was just as well. Kelli wanted to be alone.

She sat behind the big desk and surveyed the room. *Someday.* She had big ideas and even bigger dreams. It was hard to stuff them all back into the genie bottle now, but she had known it wouldn't last. Still, this sip of champagne had ruined her for beer.

Of course, she'd get to see her girls more now that the show was over. But would she see as much of Sam? He said they had things to discuss. A future together? That seemed to be what he wanted.

Kelli was smiling when the phone rang, but that didn't last for long. With only two hours left in her tenure as Danbury's acting vice president and CEO, the head of the legal department informed her that the Chicago store was being sued.

A woman had fallen in the store earlier in the week. Apparently, she'd slipped on spilled soda in women's apparel and broken one arm and both wrists trying to brace for the fall. She played violin in the Chicago

168

Symphony, meaning her livelihood would be disrupted for the duration of her recovery and rehabilitation.

"How much is her attorney seeking?" Kelli asked, rubbing her forehead. She sucked in a breath when she heard the sum.

"It seems like a lot, I know," the man on the other end of the line said. She'd met him once in a meeting and found him patronizing. He was no less so on the telephone.

"It is a lot."

"We'll fight it and most likely wind up settling with her attorney for a lot less. Don't take it to heart, Ms. Walters. These things happen no matter who is sitting in the top seat. Consider it the cost of doing business."

She hung up, feeling a little queasy.

"Are you going to miss us, Sam?" Katie asked as the two of them folded clothes and waited for Kelli to get home.

He stopped, a tiny pair of pink tights clutched in his hands. "What do you think, Katie-did?"

"Mom says it's impolite to answer a question with a question."

"She would," he mumbled.

"Well?"

"Of course, I'm going to miss you."

And he knew he meant the words. He was going

to miss the clatter of small feet; the incessant chatter, squeals and giggles that punctuated nearly every waking hour he spent with them. He was going to miss the simple joy of eating popcorn and drinking iced tea while watching a borrowed video on a small television screen. He was going to miss sticky fingers and messy kisses and construction paper artwork held to the refrigerator door with magnets.

And he was going to miss quiet, late-night conversations with the woman he'd fallen in love with. A woman he was no longer sure loved him back.

Wasn't that the kicker? he thought bitterly. He'd run far and fast from love only to have it sneak up on him. Gang up on him, really. Three to one. The odds had been in Kelli's favor all along. Had she known that? Used that? He didn't want to think she would exploit her kids for a big payout. But hadn't she always told him that they came first? That she would do whatever was necessary to ensure their future?

"You'll come see us, right?" Katie asked.

He folded one of the T-shirts Kelli used as pajamas. "It's kind of complicated."

Fat tears swam in Katie's brown eyes.

"Whenever adults say that it means no. You promised to take me to my dance, Sam. You promised!"

Sam set aside the laundry and pulled her onto his lap. Holding her close, he said, "And I will. I *always* keep my promises."

*   *   *

Joe and his daughter had removed the last of the remote cameras from Kelli's apartment. Another crew had similarly divested Sam's house of the devices. Kelli and Sam had each packed up their belongings in preparation for returning to their respective lives. Kelli had already sent the limo driver ahead with all of the clothes she'd bought for her role as CEO. Would she ever wear them again? Not for a long time. Not much call for high heels or fancy dresses in her real life.

Kelli was going to miss Sam's office and the respect she had commanded from behind his big desk, but she wasn't particularly sorry to bid farewell to his large house. It was a nice place, but she hadn't spent much time there, even though she had had a hand in decorating it, she mused, fluffing a pillow on the new couch that helped fill the great room. She walked through each of the rooms slowly, making sure everything was in its place. Maybe the house would have felt more like a home with the girls running underfoot, their fingerprints on the windows, their laughter echoing from the high ceilings. Or with Sam waiting on the couch in the evenings, greeting her with his sexy smile.

She'd made such a huge mistake with Kyle, determined to believe in a fairy-tale ending even when cold reality got in the way. Well, Sam and Kyle were nothing alike. Even the emotions they evoked in her could not be compared. She'd never felt this kind of need, this kind of love, even during the early days of her marriage.

Her eyes were wide open this time. Sam wasn't perfect, but something kept whispering that he was perfect for her. She took a deep breath and headed for the door. She planned to listen to that voice.

As usual, Sam was waiting on the couch when she got home. It wasn't late, only about seven o'clock. The girls greeted her at the door with squeals of delight, wrapping her in hugs and showering her with kisses. Sam waited patiently. And although Kelli couldn't have said why, he looked grim.

"Hello."

"Katie, can you take Chloe back to the bedroom and read her a story, please?" Sam asked. "I'd like to talk to your mother."

Katie divided a questioning gaze between the two of them before taking Chloe by the hand and leading her out of the room.

When the door clicked shut behind them, Kelli said, "I thought we were going to dinner. I stopped by Miriam Davies's apartment already and asked her if she could watch the girls."

"I want to talk to you first."

"Is something wrong?"

"I hope not. But I heard something today that really bothers me. I just need you to answer some questions."

"Okay," Kelli said slowly.

"Is there going to be a lawsuit?"

She blinked in surprise. "You already know about that?"

"I've managed to stay well-informed," Sam replied bitterly.

"It's nothing personal, the lawyer tells me. It's just the price of doing business. He said it could happen to anyone sitting in the CEO seat."

"You'd do anything for your girls, wouldn't you?"

She didn't understand the switch in topics, but she nodded. "Of course, I would. Anything."

"And to think you had me fooled." Sam shook his head. "I thought...I guess it really doesn't matter what I thought. I was wrong. Again."

"I don't understand. What are you wrong about?" Panic built as he walked toward the door. "Why are you leaving?"

"You have to ask?"

"Sam, talk to me. For heaven's sake, I don't understand what's going on here. One lawsuit against Danbury's and you're walking out the door?"

He held out a hand. A single key on a gold loop dangled from his index finger. Her apartment key. And when he said goodbye, she knew he meant forever.

Sam didn't go directly home. He drove to Stephen Danbury's house, determined to fill his boss in about the situation before he heard it from another source.

And he was prepared to offer his resignation to protect Danbury's from further liability.

Stephen's wife, Catherine, opened the door, greeting him with a warm smile. She was a beautiful woman, and so obviously in love with her husband. The feeling, of course, was returned, Sam knew. The first time he had seen the pair of them together, he'd felt a bit like an interloper. The simple glances they shared had been charged with not only sexual energy, but the kind of deep emotion that keeps couples together through good times and bad. He envied them that.

For a while there, he'd thought he might have found that kind of a connection, even though he certainly hadn't been looking for it. But, Kelli had ultimately chosen a big payday over a relationship with him.

"Stephen's in the nursery, rocking Galena. I'll go get him."

"No, please, don't disturb him. I can come back." He ran a hand around the back of his neck, cursing his preoccupation. It was well after eight o'clock. "I should have called first anyway. Forgive me for being so rude."

"Nonsense, Sam," Catherine replied. She tucked an arm through his, pulling him inside. "It's always good to see you."

She settled him in the great room and, after pouring him a drink, went to tell her husband that he had company.

"You look like a man with a lot on his mind," Stephen said. He nodded to the drink Sam held in his hand. "I could use one of those myself. If tonight is anything like last night, no one will be doing much sleeping around here."

But he smiled after he said it. And Sam understood perfectly. As exhausting as children could be, there was something ultimately rewarding about seeing to their well-being. Thinking about Kelli's children reminded him of the reason for his visit.

"I'm resigning my position effective immediately."

Glass midway to his lips, Stephen stopped and blinked. "What?"

"Sorry to just blurt that out, but I think it's for the best. Of course, I'll be happy to stay on until a replacement can be found. That is, if you want me to."

Stephen took a generous swallow of Scotch, gritted his teeth and said, "Why don't you back up a bit and tell me why you feel the need to resign? Is this because of the show? Because you were both disqualified for some reason? I'm disappointed that we won't be getting all of that free publicity, but I don't expect you to fall on your sword over it."

"It's not that. I…I don't know if you've been informed or not, but it appears there's a lawsuit."

"Yes. Kelli called this afternoon."

"She called you?" Sam asked, incredulous. "How much does she want?"

"The lawyers haven't worked it out yet." Stephen set his drink aside. "Am I missing something here? Why would you resign over a woman's slip and fall in the women's apparel department of the downtown store? Did you trip her?''

''Slip and fall?'' Sam shook his head. ''No, no, I'm talking about the sexual harassment suit.''

''Okay,'' Stephen said slowly. ''That one's news to me. Why don't you elaborate?''

Half a glass of Scotch later, Sam had finished his story. But far from looking outraged or angry, Stephen appeared skeptical.

''So, you shared a few indiscreet moments that apparently were caught on camera.''

Sam didn't appreciate having what he felt for Kelli boiled down to something so trite.

''What is, or rather *was,* going on between the two of us was far more than a few indiscreet moments.''

Stephen raised an eyebrow, but didn't comment on that. Instead he continued with his point. ''Anyway, and then you heard secondhand through Lottie that the word lawsuit came up during a conversation Lottie overheard Kelli having with Celine. Now you're resigning based on that information.''

It sounded a little silly when Stephen put it like that.

''She needs the money.''

''A lot of people need money, Sam, that doesn't make them manipulative or dishonest.''

''But she admitted to the lawsuit.''

''You specifically asked her if she was bringing a sexual harassment lawsuit against you and she said yes?''

"No, but…she's no fool, Stephen. At the very beginning, she even warned me that kissing her could court legal trouble."

Stephen raised both of his eyebrows at that.

"What exactly went on between the two of you?"

"Nothing got out of hand, but it could have if…"

Sam knew he was red as a beet, but Stephen wasn't letting him off the hook.

"Go on."

"Well, the kids, for one thing. Kind of hard to get carried away when you never know when one of them is going to wake up."

Stephen glanced toward the stairway and grimaced.

"Yeah, I know what you mean. Still, that doesn't sound like Kelli Walters. I've had quite a few conference calls and meetings with her since she's been sitting in your office, and my impression of her is that she's an upright, honest, hardworking and bright young woman. She doesn't strike me as the type to want to get something for nothing or by dishonest means."

"She had me fooled, too," Sam said bitterly.

"Catherine would say this sounds like a trust issue. Why don't you talk to Kelli, resolve things between the two of you, before you sacrifice your career?"

"I'm going to get Danbury's sued," Sam said impatiently. "That's what it's ultimately all about. A big payout. A bigger payout than even the show would have provided Kelli if she won."

"Are you sure?" Stephen asked. "Are you *abso-*

lutely sure that's all Kelli's after? I made assumptions with Catherine, too. And they almost cost me everything I now hold dear.''

They were surprising words from the man whose entire demeanor changed when he looked at his wife.

Still Sam said, ''This is different.''

''Not really. Love is about trust.''

''That obvious, huh?''

''It's written all over your face.''

''So, you won't let me quit.''

''Nope.''

''What about the no-fraternization policy? At the very least I blew that one to kingdom come.''

''It might not apply.'' Stephen shrugged and then grinned. ''Spouses are exempt.''

Kelli didn't sleep well that night. She'd gotten used to having Sam's reassuring presence on her couch. The girls must have felt the same. For the first time in months, Katie climbed into bed with her. And when she heard Chloe begin to cry around two, Kelli went and got her, too. All three of them snuggled together in the bed. They were her entire world, all she would ever need. That had been her mantra for a long time. But now, her heart told her something was missing.

Sam rolled to his side and glanced at the clock. The night was half over and he was still wide awake. For the first time in a month, he had a comfortable mattress under his back and was in a room where the temperature was perfectly regulated and humidity free. He couldn't hear car horns or the train rumbling past on its elevated tracks a couple of blocks over. He should be sleeping like a baby.

Like Chloe.

He flipped onto his stomach with a groan. And as he pictured the three blond females who had taken over his heart, he knew he wouldn't be getting any sleep that night.

CHAPTER TWELVE

NEARLY a week passed and Sam was kept so busy—or rather he'd kept himself so busy—he shouldn't have had time to even think about Kelli Walters or her girls. But he did. He hadn't taken Stephen's advice yet and asked Kelli point-blank about the lawsuit. It didn't sit well with him to admit he was afraid—afraid of what her answer might be.

He glanced around his office. Kelli had left her mark there as well. She'd brought in some plants: a large ficus in a brass pot stood sentinel near the door. It had already shed some leaves, as if weeping for its previous caretaker. And, well it should, Sam thought grimly as another leaf fluttered to the ground. He had no green thumb.

On the corner of his desk, a vase sat. The rose inside it had wilted pitifully over the past few days. Sam kept meaning to throw it away. He stood up, intending to do it now, when Lottie buzzed him.

"Yes, what is it?"

"A Miss Walters is here to see you, Mr. Maxwell. She says it's very important that she speak to you."

Kelli was here. He took a deep breath. "Send her in."

He wanted answers, and he'd have them now. He remained standing, planning to use his height to his advantage. But the person who walked through the door was not Kelli. It was Katie.

"Katie!" He glanced at his watch. "Why aren't you in school?"

"I had to see you. It's urgent."

She sounded so serious that there was no way he could smile. He nodded gravely, and motioned for her to sit in one of the chairs in front of his desk. She perched there, feet not touching the floor, and clutched a pink backpack in her arms.

"Does your mother know you've come to see me?"

Katie glanced down at her shoes. "No. I plan to be home before she has a chance to worry."

"Why don't you tell me what's so important you'd skip school to see me?"

"Well, that dance is this weekend." She squirmed in her seat. "You know, the Daddy-Daughter Dance."

Sam walked around his desk and hunkered down in front of her. Taking one of her small hands in his, he said, "Did you think I forgot?"

"No, I... You remembered?" Her face brightened.

"Of course I did. I promised."

"But I didn't think... I mean, you and my mom, well you seemed so mad at one another that last night you were home."

Home, she'd said. Not our home, just home. As if Sam had a right to call it that, too. Kids made things so simple, and so complicated.

"I keep my promises, Katie. I intend to keep this

one.'' He stood, figuring that would be the end of it and he could drive her back to school.

But she blurted out, ''I've decided not to go.''

''Did you change your mind because of your mom?''

''Sort of. She bought me this new dress,'' Katie told him, zipping open the backpack so she could pull it out.

Sam didn't know much about fashions or fabrics, but it was adorable. Pale pink and frilly, with a wide satin sash and rose buds wreathing the neckline.

''Don't you like the dress?''

''I love it,'' she replied solemnly. ''I've never owned anything so pretty. But...I know it was really expensive, even if she did get a discount since she works at Danbury's.''

Of course, Kelli would make her purchase here. He'd never known a more loyal employee. And just when he was thinking Stephen was right and he had misjudged her, Katie added, ''We don't have money for things like this.''

''Your mother must think otherwise, or she wouldn't have bought it.'' And he thought he knew exactly where she figured that money was going to come from.

''I know, but she gave her ring to some guy. I heard her tell Mrs. Murphy that his name is Mr. Pawn, and he gave her the money for it. I've decided I'd rather not go to the dance if it means my mom doesn't get to keep her ring. It's the only nice thing she's ever bought for herself. It has my birthstone and Chloe's. She bought it last Mother's Day.''

Her bottom lip trembled and so did Sam's heart. And if he hadn't already tumbled headlong in love with Kelli and her daughters, he would have done so now.

Stephen's words come back to him. Sam had made assumptions about Kelli. But no one who worshiped money would pawn her mother's ring to buy a little girl a pretty dress to attend her first dance.

He'd been wrong. More than wrong, he'd been a fool. A blind fool who'd let a past betrayal nearly destroy his future. Was it too late? It couldn't be. He wouldn't let it be.

"You keep that dress. And I want you in it when I come by to pick you up for that dance this weekend.''

"But, Sam—''

"Don't worry, Katie-did. I'll take care of it.''

And he would, he decided, more determined than he could ever remember being.

When he dropped Katie off at school forty minutes later, he reminded her, "Remember, don't mention this to your mom. I want it to be a surprise.''

Kelli took a deep breath before opening the door. She knew who would be on the other side: Sam. He was here to pick up Katie for the Daddy-Daughter Dance. Kelli was thankful for that, grateful to him that he'd remembered and realized just how important this was to a seven-year-old. But she also knew seeing him again would be pure torture.

He looked as handsome as she feared he would, impeccably dressed in a charcoal suit and crisp white shirt. In his hands he held a white florist box and a bouquet of red roses.

"Hello, Sam."

Kelli applauded herself for managing to sound normal despite her hammering pulse. Despite her aching heart.

"Hello."

"It's really nice of you to do this."

"I wanted to."

"The flowers are a nice touch, too. No one's ever brought her flowers before."

"They're not for Katie." He held out the white box to her daughter. "This is for Katie. The roses are for you."

Kelli felt her mouth fall open, but no words escaped. How long had it been since a man had brought her a dozen long-stemmed red roses? Never, she realized. No man, not even her ex-husband, had ever purchased such a bouquet for her.

Sam filled the void.

"You once told me that those red roses you buy represent hope. Well, I'm hoping you can forgive me."

"For what, exactly?" she whispered as she took the bouquet and buried her face in the fragrant blooms. "You never did tell me."

"For doubting you, for doubting myself."

She knew a moment of panic. Surely, this couldn't be happening. Surely, there was some mistake or some last roadblock to happiness. In Kelli's experience, there always was.

"W-what about the company's policy on fraternization?" she asked.

Sam took a step closer, grinning. "Stephen might be willing to change it."

"And if he won't?"

"I'll quit."

The grin was gone and she realized he was serious.

"You'd quit your job just to date me?"

"I can always find another job. There's only one you. But, to answer your question, no, I wouldn't quit my job just to date you."

"Okay, I'm confused."

"Then let me clarify things."

He pulled something from his pocket. When Kelli realized what it was her eyes filled with tears.

"My ring! How did you get it?"

"It wasn't easy. Do you know how many pawn shops there are in Chicago?" He reached out and wiped the tears from her cheeks.

Taking her hand, he said, "It's not the only ring I want to give you, Kelli Walters, but I think it will do for now."

"Oh, my God! Are you...are you proposing?"

"Clumsily, yes." When she opened her mouth to speak, Sam rushed ahead. "I know you like your independence. And I know you like doing things on your own, in your own way, but I think we make a good team.''

"Sam—"

"Hear me out. At some point in the past several weeks, I fell in love with you, but it took me a while to admit it to myself and then to trust that emotion. I want you in my life, Kelli. Not just for a little while, but forever.''

"Sam—"

"Wait, let me finish. Kyle might not have been cut out for fatherhood, but I am. I'd like to add a stone or two to this mother's ring someday, but in the meantime, I don't want to be just 'Sam' to Katie and Chloe. I want to be 'Daddy.' For keeps.''

"Can I say something now?"

Sam took a deep breath and expelled it in a rush. "Yeah, I'm all out of declarations."

"Well, I have one. And I've been saving it up for a while now. Waiting for just the right moment, I suppose. This appears to be it. I love you, too, Sam.''

The words were barely out of her mouth before she found herself in his arms, wrapped tightly there, a perfect fit.

"Looks like we're both winners after all," Kelli said on a sigh.

"Does this mean Sam is going to live here?" Katie asked and Chloe stood clapping her hands.

"Nope," Sam replied. "It means you guys are coming to live with me."

And Kelli thought she knew exactly how to decorate the rest of his big house: with love.

Harlequin Romance®

Contract Brides

From paper marriage...to wedded bliss?

A wedding dilemma:

What should a sexy, successful bachelor do if he's too busy making millions to find a wife? Or if he finds the perfect woman, and just has to strike a bridal bargain...?

The perfect proposal:

The solution? For better, for worse, these grooms in a hurry have decided to sign, seal and deliver the ultimate marriage contract...to buy a bride!

Coming Soon to

HARLEQUIN®
Romance®

featuring the favorite miniseries Contract Brides:

THE LAST-MINUTE MARRIAGE
by Marion Lennox, #3832
on sale February 2005

A WIFE ON PAPER
by award-winning author Liz Fielding, #3837
on sale March 2005

VACANCY: WIFE OF CONVENIENCE
by Jessica Steele, #3839
on sale April 2005

Available wherever Harlequin books are sold.

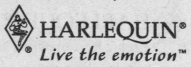

HARLEQUIN®
Live the emotion™

www.eHarlequin.com

HRCB1204

Harlequin Romance®

Every month, sample the fresh new talent in Harlequin Romance®!
For sparkling, emotional, feel-good romance, try:

January 2005
Marriage Make-Over, #3830
by *Ally Blake*

February 2005
Hired by Mr. Right, #3834
by *Nicola Marsh*

March 2005
For Our Children's Sake, #3838
by *Natasha Oakley*

April 2005
The Bridal Bet, #3842
by *Trish Wylie*

The shining new stars of tomorrow!

Available wherever Harlequin books are sold.

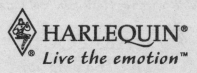

HARLEQUIN®
Live the emotion™

www.eHarlequin.com

HRNTA1204

If you enjoyed what you just read,
then we've got an offer you can't resist!

Take 2 bestselling love stories FREE!

Plus get a FREE surprise gift!

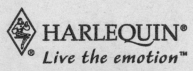